"I read what you wrote," Luke said, his voice low and sexy. "We share certain . . . otherworldly interests."

"Is that so?" Colleen asked.

"It is. Your articles were great. Intense."

She was flattered in spite of herself. "You think?"

"I know. We should talk about it sometime."

Her eyes darted nervously down the hallway again. "I have a boyfriend."

"Kevin Armour," Luke filled in. "What makes you think I have any interest in whether or not you have a boyfriend?"

Colleen flushed. "I . . . well . . ."

He took her left hand and looked at the fingers. "I don't see a wedding ring." His touch made her melt.

She pulled her hand back, flustered. Which was ridiculous. *You have lots of guy friends. Guy friends are fine.*

Not ones that make your knees go weak.

enchanted ♥ HEARTS

Love Him Forever

Cherie Bennett

AN AVON FLARE BOOK

The song lyrics found on pages 71-72, 87-88, and 101 are from Carol Ponder's CD, ''Pretty Bird: A Capella Ballads in the Southern Music Tradition.''

AVON BOOKS, INC.
1350 Avenue of the Americas
New York, New York 10019

Copyright © 1999 by Cherie Bennett and Jeff Gottesfeld
Published by arrangement with the author
Library of Congress Catalog Card Number: 99-94827
ISBN: 0-380-80124-8
www.avonbooks.com

First Avon Flare Printing: November 1999

AVON FLARE TRADEMARK REG. U.S. PAT. OFF. AND IN OTHER COUNTRIES, MARCA REGISTRADA, HECHO EN U.S.A.

Printed in the U.S.A.

WCD   10   9   8   7   6   5   4   3   2   1

For Alicia O'Brien:
You go, girl!

Love Him Forever

one
ℒ

Passionate. That was how Colleen Belmont thought of herself. Passionate was definitely good.

Tempestuous. That was how Tolliver Heath thought of her. He also thought she was volatile, unreasonable, and melodramatic. All of which were definitely bad.

As Tolliver pontificated to the staff of The *Lakesider*, the oh-so-imaginatively-named student newspaper of Lakeside High School, Colleen raised her index finger into the air. She knew Tolliver was watching her, because he was always watching her. The editor in chief had the world's hugest crush on Colleen, and everyone knew it.

He stopped mid-sentence. "Yes, Colleen?"

She smiled at him sweetly. Her loathing for him didn't show a bit. "Well, Tollie," she began, "remember our discussion at last week's editorial meeting about my proposed new paranormal phenomena column for the paper?"

"Yes, what of it?" Tollie resettled his glasses on his skinny nose. He was tall and so thin that his expensive clothes hung on his body as if it were a coat rack. No one had ever seen him in jeans. The entire newspaper staff had an ongoing betting pool—a con-

1

firmed sighting of Tollie in jeans was worth fifty bucks.

So far, no one had come close to collecting.

Tolliver, or Tollie, as he insisted he be called, ran editorial meetings of the school paper like they were Strategic Air Command crisis strategy sessions for global thermonuclear war. Colleen was sure he had never cracked a joke in his entire life. And she seriously doubted he had actual bodily functions.

"Well, Tollie," Colleen went on sweetly, "I've taken the liberty of writing up a few samples of the column—I'm thinking of calling it 'Beyond Reason'— and I thought we could try one out in next week's issue of the paper." She got up and handed a few sheets of paper to Tolliver.

"That's a great idea!" Betsy Wu exclaimed. She was Colleen's best friend and the newspaper's sports reporter. "This school could stand a little excitement. I vote we give it a try."

Tolliver gave Betsy a contemptuous look. "Might I point out that you haven't even read the samples yet."

"They're Colleen's," Betsy said with a shrug. "She's the best writer on the paper, so they must be great."

"And here I thought Celeste was the best writer on this paper," Brandon Marrow joked. He was a junior who covered music and dance.

"Please don't mention the Curls," Betsy said. "She's out sick, and I for one am thrilled with the reprieve."

"Might we stick to the subject at hand, people?" Tolliver asked.

"We might, Tollie, my man," Kevin Armour replied. "Colleen's idea is great. I say we go for it."

Colleen smiled radiantly in Kevin's direction.

Big mistake. Tollie's nostrils twitched. That was never good.

You know you can never, ever show attention to any other guy in front of Tolliver, Colleen admonished herself, *even if Tollie knows you are going out with the guy to whom you're showing attention, because Tolliver's maggot-size ego can't take the comp.*

And she wouldn't have slipped up if it hadn't been for the fact that she knew Kevin actually detested her paranormal column idea. She'd just been completely surprised when he'd publicly supported it anyway.

Colleen and Kevin had been a couple for almost a year. Kevin's parents were both involved in the theater, and they had moved to Milwaukee from their home in New York City to do a year-long residency at the University of Wisconsin's Milwaukee campus and to work at Milwaukee Repertory Theatre. Kevin was much more interested in photography—he was the number-one news photographer for the *Lakesider*.

Even Betsy, who had been brutal on all of Colleen's previous boyfriends (of whom there had been exactly three since seventh grade), thought they made a great couple. Lots of people said Kevin resembled the tennis player Peter Sampras. He had Sampras's thick, curly, dark hair; electric, dark eyes; and easy, open grin. He habitually had a camera, and sometimes two, around his neck, and was forever telling Colleen that what he cared about was what *was*, not what *might be.* That was woo-woo stuff, as he called it. He was the ultimate skeptic.

Colleen, on the other hand, was, if not the ultimate believer, at least the ultimate in open-mindedness. Her Ouija board had been her favorite Christmas gift when she was ten, and she used the same board now to commune with what she called "Other Worlds."

She had the classic petite Irish good looks of her mother, who had come to the United States from Dublin as a little girl. Her bright-red, wavy hair was her trademark—it reached down nearly to the bottom of her back. Her skin was pale and beautiful, her eyes were an intense shade of blue, and she was famous for the antique pins she collected from garage sales and thrift shops.

Colleen loved to write, especially about movies. Her goal was to replace Roger Ebert as the movie critic at the *Chicago Sun-Times*. She was pretty confident she could do it, too.

So was everyone else.

What she wasn't confident about was whether or not she could get through high school without strangling Tolliver Heath's scrawny chicken-skinned neck. He was utterly, royally, dictatorial and unfair. She *hated* that.

Tolliver sighed. "Colleen, this is a school newspaper, not a tabloid supermarket scandal sheet full of made-up supernatural garbage."

"My column would not be supernatural garbage, as you so eloquently put it, Tollie," Colleen retorted. She could feel herself getting angrier, the color rising to her cheeks.

Chill, she told herself. *You've worked so hard to keep your temper in check lately. You can do it, you can do it, you can do it. You know you can do it.*

"There's more and more research being done in this area, and important discoveries are being made almost every day," she said, keeping her voice even. "All I'm asking is that you look at my sample articles, Tollie. Please?"

"Come on, Tol," Kevin urged him. "You know Colleen rocks, so give her a break."

Bad move. Tollie's nostrils quivered like Jell-O in an earthquake.

"I would have to have rocks in my head to approve this swill," Tollie replied, shuffling through Colleen's articles. " 'Ouija and Your SATs'? 'How to Change Your Aura in Sixty Seconds'? 'Past Life Regression for High School Students in Five Easy Steps'?" He threw the articles onto the desk. "May I vomit now, or shall I wait until later?"

Colleen's face grew redder. "It so happens I asked my Ouija board what the big essay question was going to be on our history final last marking period. And I seem to recall I aced that test—"

"Unlike someone we know," Betsy put in, and pushed a strand of bright green hair out of her face. Very petite, with a round face and beautiful almond-shaped eyes, her alternative style was legendary. At the moment she wore a long bottle-green plaid skirt with an oversized orange-and-red sweater, one of her more conservative looks. She'd added a streak of red and a streak of green to her hair, in honor of it being the month of Christmas.

Tolliver shot Betsy a dirty look. He'd gotten a B in history last marking period, the very first B of his life. If that wasn't bad enough, everyone had made buzzing noises around him for more than a week afterward. He'd been so depressed that it had taken days for him to realize they were buzzing like a bee. Ha-ha.

"That B was a tiny stitch in the fabric of my life," Tolliver huffed. "The fact remains that these—*your*—so-called columns are not fit to run in my newspaper.

Not now, not tomorrow, and not forever, not in any paper of which I am in charge.''

''But—'' Colleen began.

Tolliver ignored her. ''Now, since we are, by my calculations, two minutes behind, we'll move on to the next order of business, the publicity for our College Bowl team. The team will be—''

''You're not even going to take them home to read them through?'' Colleen asked.

''I prioritize, Colleen,'' Tollie informed her. ''Jokes such as your column make my list somewhere under 'Extra Time Spent Dental Flossing.' Now, where was I? Ah, yes. The College Bowl team is—''

''—about as interesting as the last editorial you wrote,'' Colleen broke in. Her cheeks were flaming now, but she didn't care. ''I mean, please, Tolliver, you think we should return to the dress code of the nineteen-fifties? No one in the entire school but you owns the wardrobe for it!''

''This is great,'' Brandon muttered gleefully. The entire staff was watching, grins on their faces. They never interrupted a good fight between Tollie and Colleen. It was always the best part of an editorial meeting. A couple of them even formed their hands into the shape of guns and blew imaginary smoke away from the tips of their index fingers.

Yikes, Betsy thought. *Bad move, Colleen. Criticize anything you want about Tolliver, but don't criticize his editorials.*

''Although it was an interesting point of view,'' Betsy called to Tollie, hoping to rescue her friend.

Tollie never even heard her. He glared at Colleen. ''Let me remind you my editorial was submitted by the administration to the National Board of Student

Newspapers for the Best Editorial of the Year Award.''

"Big duh, Tollie," Colleen replied. "Our principal went to high school in the fifties, which is the last time he had anything resembling a life. That was a suck-up editorial and you know it, Tolliver. You just want that award for your application to Yale."

Kevin groaned and slumped in his seat. Betsy shook her head sadly. They'd both seen Colleen's mouth get the better of her too many times. She could never stand by silently when someone was treating someone else unfairly. Especially if the someone was her.

Tolliver leaned over the table toward Colleen. She could see the little hairs inside his quivering nostrils. It wasn't pretty. "I am staying calm because I am a professional," he told her. "Now, for the last time, no insipid occult column. We only print stories of real interest to our peers. And that's final!"

"Cool," Betsy agreed, hoping to end the conversation. "So, moving on to that swell College Bowl thingie—"

Colleen stood up and leaned toward Tolliver. "You don't think our peers care more about the paranormal than they did about your weenie editorial?" she challenged. "What was it that happened the day after your brilliant editorial ran? Right, now I remember. Everyone came to school dressed in Tolliver Heath–approved bow ties."

"And they weren't so easy to find, Tollie, I gotta tell you," Brandon pointed out. "I looked all over Milwauk—"

Tolliver slammed his palm on the table. Colleen jumped. His eyes grew cold. They bore into hers. "Don't push me, Colleen."

For just a moment, she thought he looked scary. Like, really, *really* scary. But that was just her vivid imagination. This was Tolliver Heath, she reminded herself, not the hook guy from *I Still Know What You Did Last Summer*.

"And don't you push me, Tollie," Colleen replied. "I'm not going to pretend that you're making this decision in the best interests of the paper. Because you're not."

"As editor in chief, I—"

"Here's three chords and the truth, Tollie," Colleen interrupted. "You're not going to win this time."

The room was so quiet they could all hear the cheerleaders practicing in the gym at the other end of the school. Tolliver composed himself. He hated being out of control. And he didn't dare to push Colleen off the newspaper. For one thing, she was the best writer he had. And for another . . .

Well. That was private.

"I'll overlook your behavior this time," Tolliver said, pushing at his glasses. "Now, we have—"

"Wow, look at the time." Colleen grabbed her backpack and headed for the door. "I almost forgot, the new Spielberg movie's opening at the Cinema Center today."

"But what about the rest of the meet—"

"Sorry, Tollie, guess I've got to go review it. You wouldn't want me to have an empty space where my movie column would be, would you? Or would you rather we just pop in one of those occult articles? I didn't think so."

Tolliver stood there, helpless, as she walked out of the newspaper office and clicked the door closed behind her. There was really nothing he could say. After all, she *was* the paper's movie critic, and the new movie *was* opening. She was merely doing her job. He sat down and shuffled his papers. He was way past quivering nostrils. Now his hands shook, and his jaw was clenched so tightly the veins stood out in his neck.

Betsy leaned toward Kevin. "Score: Belmont, one; Heath, goose egg."

"Never get cocky about the score in the second inning, I always say," Kevin replied. Lately something about Heath had been giving him the creeps. "If I know Tollie, he's going to try to get back at her. Soon."

Colleen was lost in thought at her computer. She'd been writing, but her mind had begun to wander. When she left the newspaper meeting that afternoon, she'd almost run headlong into Luke Ransom. He was new, a senior who had moved to Lakeside from New Orleans. His eyes were light blue, his chin chiseled, his body lanky, his walk sinewy. Colleen had never even spoken to him. But sometimes she would feel this heat, and she'd turn around, and those blue, blue eyes would be staring at her, through her, seeing everything.

Yeah, right. She shook off the feeling. Her vivid imagination was just getting the best of her, that was all. So the guy was hot. Lots of guys were hot. She was in love with Kevin.

She forced herself to concentrate on her writing, and began typing again. Someone knocked on her door.

"Go away," she called out, and kept typing.

"Aren't you even going to ask who it is?" her little sister, Kat, demanded through the door.

"I know who it is," Colleen replied.

"Can I come in?"

"No. I'm working."

"On what?"

"On none of your business."

"What's none of my business?" Kat called back.

Colleen groaned and began counting down from the number ten silently. *She's going to be through that door by the time I reach six,* she thought to herself. *Ten, nine, eight*—

The door popped open, and Kat stuck her head in. Her dark ponytail poked through the back of her baseball cap, and she wore a red, white, and blue Davis Cup–style warm-up suit. Only eleven, Kat was a ranked tennis player not only in her own age group in the state of Wisconsin but also in the under-14 category.

"Well, what a surprise to have you just walk in after I asked you nicely to go away," Colleen said.

Kat plopped down on Colleen's bed and bounced up and down. "You didn't ask nicely. You asked meanly."

"It's really too bad your maturity on the court doesn't extend to the rest of your life," Colleen said. "Stop bouncing."

Kat stopped by popping up from the bed onto her feet. She went to peer over her sister's shoulder at the computer screen. Colleen quickly hit a key to black it out.

"No fair!" Kat cried. "What were you writing, porno?"

Colleen gave her a withering look.

Kat shrugged. "Okay, be like that. I only came up here to tell you that tall, dark, and dorky is downstairs."

This was Kat's usual description of Kevin, whom she actually thought was so cute she could hardly breathe around him.

"Why didn't you say so?" Colleen asked, quickly backing up what she'd just written.

"I just did. Hey, can I hang out with you guys?" Kat bent over and ostentatiously began stretching out her hamstrings. "That is, after I give you five minutes for spit swapping and stuff."

Colleen got up. "No, you cannot hang out with us."

"Why not?"

"Because I said so. Kevin came over to read something that I wrote."

"Can I read it, too?"

"No." Colleen headed for the stairs. "Go study. When Mom and Dad get home, they'll want to check your math."

"I hate math. It's stupid." She hung over the banister and called down to Colleen. "What does a professional tennis player need with math, anyway, except to count money?"

Colleen ignored her and went into the living room, where Kevin was looking through one of Kat's tennis magazines.

He is so cute, she thought. He looked up and gave her a heart-melting grin.

"Hi," he said softly. "How was the movie?"

She sat next to him on the couch "What movie?" she asked. "I thought we could see it together this weekend. I just said that to get Tolliver's undies in a wad. Boxers, not briefs, I'm sure."

Kevin laughed. "Well, it worked. You were brilliant at the meeting. I mean, it was futile, empty, and senseless. But you won."

"I know I shouldn't fight with him," Colleen admitted.

"True."

"It's counterproductive to my goals."

Kevin nodded. "Also true."

"But I just—"

As Colleen said "can't help myself," Kevin said "can't help yourself," and they both laughed. She leaned over and kissed his cheek softly.

He reached for her, then stopped. "Is Kat still upstairs?"

"I told her to do math."

"Parents?"

"Out."

"Good." His steely dark eyes searched hers. The first time he had done that, when they'd first kissed back in February, she'd felt an electric rush through her entire body. His heat had melted her. And then his kisses made her burst into flames.

They still did.

His lips met hers. Softly at first, then more insistently. Eyes closed, she lost herself in the bliss of his kisses.

Oh, Luke . . .

Colleen gasped and opened her eyes. Thank God she hadn't said aloud what she'd been thinking. Kevin would never, ever forgive her if she moaned out another guy's name when he was kissing her. She loved Kevin. And she loved his kisses. So why was she thinking about—

"Hey, are you okay?" Kevin asked.

"Fine," she assured him. "Where were we?"

"Oh, about here." He brought his lips to the pulse in her throat and kissed her so softly, she shivered. "Hey, I want to talk about your birthday."

"And I want you to do that again, only on my lips," Colleen said, reaching for him.

He smiled. "It's in a month, right?"

"January first, same as last year, thirty days from today." She leaned forward and began to kiss him again.

He kissed her lightly. "How about a birthday brunch at the Adams Mark? That is, after we spend New Year's Eve together."

"Sure, sounds great. More kissing."

From the top of the stairs, Kat peered down. The hallway was empty. Good. That meant her sister was probably sucking face with tall, dark, and dorky in the living room. Which was just the opportunity Kat needed.

She darted into Colleen's room and hit the enter key on the computer so that the screen would come up again. Anytime her sister told her she couldn't do something, it made her want to do it even more. Colleen had certainly not wanted Kat to see what she was writing. Well, Kat was about to see it, anyway.

The screen filled. Kat read it quickly.

And then she screamed.

two
♫

"I'm telling." Kat spooned more oatmeal into her mouth.

"There's nothing to tell," Colleen said, taking a gulp of her orange juice.

"Is, too. What I read on your computer last night—"

"Was private," Colleen said firmly. "You had no right to read it. And you only screamed so Kevin would run upstairs to make sure you were okay because you have a crush on him."

"I do not!" Kat's face turned bright red. "I screamed because what you wrote was so weird."

Kat looked across the table at her father, whose head was, as usual, buried behind the morning *Journal-Sentinel*. CNBC business news droned in the background, on a kitchen TV that was only turned on during weekday breakfasts. "Daddy, Colleen wrote creepy stuff about people dying on her computer."

"Hm-um," their father mumbled. The newspaper rattled.

"Not just dead people," Kat went on. "Live people who go back and find out who they were before they died. It was so creepy. She's probably in a cult."

"Hm-um," their father mumbled again. He was an investment adviser and worked at a large firm in

14

downtown Milwaukee. When he read the business section of the newspaper, he tuned out the rest of the world.

"Daddy, don't you care that Colleen's brain has been taken over by—"

"Kindly shut up," Colleen told her sister.

"*You* shut up."

Their father's eyes peered at them over the top of the newspaper. "Girls, please hold it down to a dull roar. The financial news is bad enough this morning."

"Is Mom still upstairs?" Colleen asked her father.

"Yes." Mr. Belmont took a sip of his coffee.

"She's meeting with my principal today," Kat informed Colleen. "They're discussing how to deal with the prodigy that is me. And after school she's taking me to practice."

Their mom was a guidance counselor at the same junior high where Kat was in seventh grade, so it wasn't surprising that Kat knew her schedule for the day. Still, Colleen was sometimes jealous of her younger sister's closeness with their mother. Of course, you couldn't be a tennis prodigy without a parent who was willing to drive you from practice to lessons to tournaments and back again. But it wasn't like Colleen had a matching closeness with her father.

"So, Daddy, if Colleen goes back in time, can I do it, too?" Kat asked.

"No," her father said. He checked his watch and hastily sipped the last of his coffee. Then he kissed both of his daughters, grabbed his briefcase, yelled a good-bye upstairs to his wife, and headed out the door.

"No one lets me do anything," Kat whined, mushing her spoon into her now-cold oatmeal.

"You can do something," Colleen said, carrying her dishes to the sink. "Load the dishwasher. It's your turn."

Kat narrowed her eyes at her big sister. "Boy, I hope you find out you were an evil, mean, ugly witch in your last lifetime. Oh, wait, that's what you are in *this* lifetime."

"Did I hear you say 'last lifetime'?" Mrs. Belmont asked, walking briskly into the kitchen. She'd been up since five in the morning, as was her habit, and had already run three miles in the icy Wisconsin morning air, showered, and eaten her breakfast. This was her morning routine, and she followed it religiously, unless it was snowing so hard that she couldn't see her hand in front of her face.

"Colleen's going back in time to see who she was before she was Colleen," Kat explained as she began to load the dishwasher. "She's writing this article about it. It's so creepy and weird."

"It's called past life regression," Colleen said, leaning against the kitchen cabinets. "It's perfectly legitimate. Betsy's doing it, too."

Mrs. Belmont poured herself a cup of coffee and smiled at her elder daughter. Colleen had always been fascinated by the supernatural and the paranormal. But she was so eminently sane and levelheaded, and she got such good grades, that it was clear to Mrs. Belmont that her interest in the otherworldly was pretty harmless.

"Sounds interesting," Mrs. Belmont said. "Kat, sweetie, you need to scrape the oatmeal out of that bowl before you put it in the dishwasher."

Just then the doorbell rang.

"It's Betsy," Colleen said, heading for the door.

"Her mom's car broke down, so I told her we could give her a ride to school."

Betsy blew into the Belmont kitchen with her usual burst of energy. She wore plaid polyester bell-bottoms with a fuzzy thrift store sweater, and managed to make the outfit look like the height of alternative fashion.

"Starving does not begin to cover it," she said as she headed for the refrigerator and rummaged around for food. "All we have in our house is tofu and oranges. Someone report my parents to the Child Welfare Department." She grabbed a cup of cherry yogurt, got out a spoon, and leaned against the counter to eat.

"Hey, can I do past life regression with you guys?" Kat asked Betsy as she put her now-scraped dish into the dishwasher.

"Nope," Betsy replied. "My sister doesn't regress anyone younger than fifteen."

"Roni does past life regressions?" Mrs. Belmont asked.

Betsy nodded, and licked some yogurt off her spoon. "She's really into it."

The Belmonts had known the Wu family, and Roni Wu, for years. Roni was ten years older than Betsy. She had a master's degree in psychology and counseling from the University of Chicago and was working on her doctorate at Northwestern.

"Well, I feel better about it, knowing Roni's the one doing it," Mrs. Belmont said. "But please tell your older sister to be careful with my daughter. I don't want her stuck on the *Titanic* or anything."

Betsy laughed. "Wow, that would be out there, huh?"

Kat's eyes grew huge. "Stuff like that can't happen, can it?"

"No, silly," Betsy assured her, pulling on Kat's ponytail. "It's perfectly safe. Hey, maybe if you went back in time you'd find out that Kevin was your boyfriend in your last lifetime."

Kat made a face. "Tall, dark, and dorky? Gag me." She turned on the dishwasher.

"You have a huge crush on him and you know it," Betsy said, throwing away the empty yogurt container.

"I do not." Kat scowled. "Can we get going, Mom?"

"Sure, sweetie." Mrs. Belmont put her coffee cup in the sink. "So, when does this regression take place?"

"This weekend," Colleen replied. "When Roni comes back from Chicago." She looped her backpack over one shoulder.

"You'll have to give me the full report," her mother said. "It sounds kind of exciting, actually."

"Is Kevin doing it, too?" Kat asked, trying to sound nonchalant.

"Why don't you call him and ask him?" Betsy teased.

"As if!" Kat huffed. She hurried out of the kitchen.

"Stop teasing her about Kevin, Bets," Colleen said. "Don't you remember what it's like to be eleven and have a crush on an older guy?"

"My cousin Alex," Betsy admitted. "I wrote him seven thousand love letters, all still in a shoebox in my closet."

"Can we please leave in this lifetime?" Kat yelled from the hallway.

Colleen looked over at her mother. "Does Kat have to be so obnoxious all the time?"

"Better be nice to her," Mrs. Belmont advised. "Maybe she's only the little sister in *this* lifetime."

Colleen spun the combination on her locker, lost in thought. She had to find a way to get Tolliver to start her paranormal column. But this morning he'd been just as adamant about it as he had been the day before. There had to be some way to—

"Hi."

Colleen turned around. Standing there was Luke Ransom, looking so hot her knees felt weak. Something about his eyes seemed so familiar to her. As if she knew him. Maybe he felt it, too, and that was why she caught him staring at her sometimes.

No. That was crazy.

"Hi," she said. She got out her chemistry book and slammed her locker shut.

"I'm Luke Ransom."

She nodded. "I know."

"Well, I'm flattered, then," he said. "And you're Colleen Belmont." He pointed one finger at her, an amused look in his eye. "And you should be flattered, too."

Colleen shook her red hair off her face. "Frankly, I don't flatter that easily. Well, nice to have met you, Luke."

He held up his palms and laughed. "Okay, you think that was a real egotistical thing for me to say. I guess it didn't come out right. I was just kidding around."

She shrugged.

"Let me just ask you a question, Colleen Belmont. How many fingers am I holding up?" He made a peace sign with his right hand.

"Two would be the correct answer," Colleen said.

"Great. Then I'm not invisible." He leaned his shoulder lazily against her locker.

Not hardly, Colleen thought. *You're like walking fire, walking hot, sizzling, dangerous—*

"It's the new guy thing," Luke explained. "When you're the new guy, you feel kinda invisible."

"It must be tough to be new for your senior year," she acknowledged.

He nodded. "You want to connect with someone. Know that feeling?"

"Sure." She held her book to her chest and was careful not to let her eyes meet his.

"And somehow . . . well, sometimes you just feel drawn to a certain person." His eyes caught hers.

"Uh huh." She winced. Colleen Belmont, the girl with the mouth, could not think of a single thing to say.

He pulled some crumpled papers from the back pocket of his jeans and held them out to her.

"What?" she asked him.

"Your name is on these. I thought you might want them."

She took the pages. They were the crumpled-up sample columns about the paranormal she'd written for the *Lakesider*. That cretin Tolliver had apparently thrown them out without ever reading them.

"Thanks," Colleen said to him. She stuck the papers into the back of her chemistry book. "Where did you find them?"

He didn't answer her question. Instead, he touched one finger to the antique cameo pin she had pinned to her sweater. "That's beautiful."

She lowered her eyes to it. She'd found it in a thrift

shop near Marquette University. It looked to be very old. There was a small dot under the right eye of the cameo's face. Kevin insisted it was just some kind of flaw, which was why Colleen had gotten the pin so cheap, but Colleen thought it looked as if the cameo was crying.

"She's crying," Luke added.

Colleen got shivers up her spine.

"It's funny," he went on, "how much of life we don't have any control over. It's like it controls us, you know?"

She looked away. *I'm okay if I just don't look into his eyes,* Colleen told herself. *Every time I look into his eyes I feel like demanding that he kiss me this very instant. Kiss me and kiss me and—*

"Lost in thought?" he asked.

Those eyes. Stop it, Colleen.

She forced herself to sound as disinterested as possible. "I'm just preoccupied right now," she told him. "What did you say, something about control over life?" She cast a quick look over her shoulder to see if Kevin was walking down the hall from behind her. No Kevin. Good.

"I read what you wrote," Luke said, his voice low and sexy. "We share certain . . . otherworldly interests."

"Is that so?" Colleen asked.

"It is. Your articles were great. Intense."

She was flattered in spite of herself. "You think?"

"I know. We should talk about it sometime."

Her eyes darted nervously down the hallway again. "I have a boyfriend."

"Kevin Armour," Luke filled in. "What makes you think I have any interest in whether or not you have a boyfriend?"

Colleen flushed. "I . . . well . . ."

He took her left hand and looked at the fingers. "I don't see a wedding ring." His touch made her melt.

She pulled her hand back, flustered. Which was ridiculous. *You have lots of guy friends. Guy friends are fine.*

Not ones that make your knees go weak.

"I . . . I have to go," she managed, backing away from him. "To lunch."

"Ah. Lunch." He gave her a small, mocking bow. "Until we meet again, Colleen Belmont. Just like we met before."

Before she could ask him what he meant, he was gone. In the nick of time, too, since Kevin came up behind her no more than ten seconds later and planted a warm kiss on her neck.

"No PDAs," Colleen warned him. But she gave him a warm hug.

At the far end of the hall, Luke Ransom had stopped and turned back. As Kevin hugged her, her eyes met Luke's.

Luke held up his left hand and pointed to his ring finger.

No wedding ring, Colleen.

She turned her back on Luke. And though she had been the one who made the rule against public displays of affection, she held Kevin as if she was afraid to ever let him go.

three
ⅅ

"*It's a simple concept, really,*" Roni told Colleen. "*I'll* hypnotize you, we'll see a past life inside your soul, and then you'll wake up."

"That doesn't sound so simple," Kevin muttered darkly.

It was Saturday afternoon. Colleen, Kevin, Betsy, and Betsy's sister, Roni, were all in Betsy's room, preparing for Colleen's first past life regression. Roni had wanted Colleen to be in a place that was comfortable and secure to her. Colleen had spent so much time in Betsy's room over the years that it was like an extension of her own home.

Kevin had come along reluctantly, not really wanting to encourage Colleen in yet another of her woo-woo projects. But he also felt protective of her. Although Roni had assured them that nothing bad could happen, he wanted to be with Colleen, just in case.

"This isn't brain surgery, Kevin," Roni assured him briskly. She looked a lot like an older version of Betsy, but her style and personality were so different from her little sister's that they barely seemed related. At the moment, Betsy wore superbaggy jeans and a cropped bowling shirt. Roni wore a beige pantsuit and flats. Colleen wore sweats, since Roni had told her it was important that she be dressed in clothes that didn't bind her in any way.

"It won't even take that long," Colleen added.

At least that's what she had read in Raymond Moody's book *Coming Back*, all about past life regression. Betsy had loaned the book to her earlier in the week. She gave Kevin a reassuring smile and tried to hide her own nerves.

"How do you even know it will work?" Kevin asked.

"I don't," Roni said. "It doesn't always. But it will with Colleen."

"How do you know?" Colleen asked skeptically. "I don't give in to other people's wills very easily, you know."

Roni smiled. "Let's just say that intense type A personalities who think they can't be hypnotized are often the best subjects of all."

"Colleen? Intense?" Betsy feigned shock.

"What if she doesn't wake up?" Kevin asked.

Roni laughed, and Betsy joined in. "I'm a qualified hypnotherapist, and past life regression has been well studied. No one has ever not woken up."

"There's a first time for everything," Kevin said.

Colleen squeezed his hand. "It's okay, Kevin."

Kevin got up from Betsy's bed. "You don't know that, Col. What if this woo-woo stuff of yours turns out to be dangerous instead of just stupid?"

Colleen fought her mounting irritation. She was starting to feel sorry that she had invited him to be there. "You know Roni would never do anything to hurt me," she told him. "This is perfectly safe."

"Negativity isn't helpful, Kevin," Roni told him.

He folded his arms. "If she does go into some . . . some past life, how do you know that whatever she says isn't just something she's inventing?"

"I wouldn't do that!" Colleen exclaimed.

"I don't mean consciously," Kevin added quickly. "But you do have a vivid imagination, Col."

"Kevin, the Western world doesn't have a monopoly on reality, you know," Roni said. She checked the subdued lighting aimed at Betsy's bed one last time to make sure it wasn't too bright.

"Meaning what?" Kevin asked.

"Meaning that a good part of the world believes in reincarnation," Roni said, "whether you do or not."

"There's no scientific proof," Kevin replied. "Just because people believe something doesn't make it so. Or else the world used to be flat."

"You can't prove everything with the scientific method, you know," Colleen told him. "Some things just . . . just . . . happen."

Like Luke Ransom, she thought, her breath quickening.

"Like what?" Kevin asked skeptically.

Some things just . . . just . . . happen.

"Nothing," Colleen said quickly. She gave him a quick kiss. "Now, sit down and think positive thoughts, please."

"Look at it this way," Betsy told him, "if we were living in India and you didn't believe in reincarnation, you'd be the strange one, not us."

"Well, we live in America," Kevin said, clearly agitated. "Not India. And I have a bad feeling about this."

He went to the window and looked out onto the Wus' backyard, which sloped gently down to the shoreline of Lake Michigan. From the window, the lake

25

was so big it could easily be mistaken for the ocean. Down on the lakefront, supported on wooden pilings, was the Wus' old-fashioned boathouse. Until recently, Mr. Wu had kept his pride and joy, a restored Gar Wood speedboat, in that boathouse. But that fall the Wus had turned the boathouse into a sort of waterfront rec room, and Mr. Wu had reluctantly moved his boat to a nearby marina.

Colleen went to Kevin. "Look, I appreciate that you think you're looking out for me, I really do. But I'm fine. Really."

"I'd really like to start," Roni said, looking at her watch.

"Just a sec," Colleen told her. She turned to Kevin. "What if I could prove that reincarnation exists? Would that make you feel better?"

Kevin turned around. "Try me."

"Do you know what xenoglossy is?" she asked him.

"Xeno what?" Kevin asked.

"Xenoglossy," she repeated. "What if I told you that there are at least a thousand children on the planet who have been found to be speaking languages that *they never learned*?"

Kevin raised his eyebrows. "How do you know that?"

"Because it's been recorded," Roni put in. "For example, about seventy years ago, some parents brought their two kids to the linguistics school at Columbia University because they seemed to be communicating with each other in some strange language."

Kevin shrugged. "It was a hoax."

"Wrong," Roni told him. "It turned out that the kids were speaking perfect Aramaic."

"Then the parents were Aramaic," Kevin deduced. "And they spoke Aramaic when they thought their kids weren't listening. The kids picked it up."

Roni laughed. "Doubtful. Because the parents—I think they were named McDuffie—didn't know Aramaic. And that's because Aramaic is a *dead language*. It used to be spoken in parts of the Middle East . . . about two thousand years ago."

Colleen shuddered, even though the story of the McDuffie kids had been in the book she had read. But hearing Roni tell it, well, that just made the story so . . . so . . . *real*.

Kevin looked from Roni, to Betsy, to Colleen. They all looked deadly serious. "Oh, come on, you can't all be taken in by this stuff."

"You hear hoofbeats, you think horses, not zebras," Roni said. "If these kids didn't learn Aramaic from their parents, who do you think they learned it from?"

"Past li-i-i-ives," Betsy moaned in a spooky voice, just to tease him. "And who were *you* before, Kevin Armour?"

"Very funny," Kevin said, shaking his head.

"Okay, let's get started." Roni nodded at Colleen.

Colleen gave Kevin's hand a quick squeeze, then went to get comfortable on Betsy's bed.

"Good, Colleen," Roni told her. "You get relaxed." She checked the video camera one last time, then hesitated. She turned to Kevin. "I'm sorry, but I'm going to have to ask you to leave."

"But why?" Kevin demanded as Colleen sat up again. She had a funny feeling but couldn't place it. She really wanted him to stay.

"Can't he stay?" she found herself asking Roni.

"It would be a waste of time," Roni said. "Both

mine and yours. Hypnotism requires complete relaxation on the part of the subject and the hypnotist. I know you love Kevin, Colleen, but his attitude is clear, and his presence won't be helpful to your experience.''

Kevin glared at Roni, then looked at Colleen.

"Col?" he asked.

Her face burned as she tried to decide what to do.

"Forget it." He picked up his gym bag.

"Don't leave mad, Kevin," Colleen pleaded.

"I'm not. This is clearly not my scene." He turned to Roni. "Make sure you take great care of her or you'll answer to me. Got it?"

"Got it," Roni assured him.

"I love it when you get all macho like that, Kevin," Betsy teased.

Kevin laughed in spite of himself. He gave Colleen a quick kiss. "Good luck. Call me later. And if you run into Christopher Columbus, give him my regards.''

Colleen breathed deeply, so deeply. Her arms, her legs, her chest, everything felt so heavy, so languid; the most lovely warmth in the world enveloped her, caressed her, and transported her.

"Now, Colleen, I want you to feel the calm feelings in your left foot. All the way through that foot. Relax," Roni said, her voice low and soothing.

Colleen felt her left foot get heavier.

"Even more relaxed now," Roni said. "Rest."

Colleen rested.

For the previous ten minutes, Roni's soothing words had guided Colleen into a profound state of relaxation. It was the oddest experience. Colleen didn't feel like she was in a trance, exactly. More like the most peaceful state she'd ever been in.

"Rest," Roni said again. "You are completely rested, safe, and relaxed. You are feeling more deeply restful. Now, I will count you down from the number eight, and with each number, I want you to feel even more rested. Deeply, deeply rested. Eight."

Colleen felt the last tensions of her life leave her body.

"Seven. Six. Five. Four. You're more relaxed, more calm than you have ever been."

Colleen wanted to nod, but her head felt too heavy.

"Three. Very relaxed. Two. Very, very relaxed. And one."

Colleen's chest rose and fell slowly, evenly. The feeling she had was the same one she'd had the previous summer, when she and Kevin had spent a glorious afternoon on one of the beaches at the lake. It had been a perfect day, no one had been around, and the two of them had laid on a towel in their swimsuits, hand in hand, and Colleen had felt safer than she had ever felt in her life.

Roni told Colleen to picture herself in some safe place, a relaxed and safe place. But Colleen was already there, on the beach, with Kevin.

Then Roni told her to rise up out of her body, out of the room, out of the house, to the safe place.

Colleen knew, on one level, that what Roni was telling her was impossible.

And yet, in her mind, she did it. She could see herself, and Kevin, together on that safe beach. A smile curled her lips.

"Now, Colleen," Roni's voice said soothingly, "you are going to come back to earth. But when you are back on earth, you will find yourself in a previous life, one that you have already lived, before you were Colleen. You will live this life, you will see the scenes, and you will be able to talk to me about them.''

Again, Colleen wanted to nod, but her head felt too heavy. What Roni was telling her made perfect sense. And it seemed so easy, so natural.

"Accept what you see, Colleen," Roni's voice went on, "and tell me what you see. You are completely safe. You are completely, completely safe."

"Safe," Colleen barely whispered.

"Yes, safe," Roni assured her. "Feel yourself float down to earth now, Colleen. Safely and serenely, no worries, you float down to earth."

Down.

Down.

Down.

Down.

Contact. She was standing on something.

Colleen looked around.

She was in a city. The buildings looked familiar to her, in a way, but they were also strange.

"What do you see?" She could hear Roni's voice, even though she was in this city.

"Buildings," Colleen whispered.

"Explore them," Roni urged. "Feel free to move around."

Colleen looked around. The buildings were modern, in a way—not as modern as those in Milwaukee, true, but not from long, long, ago, either. More things came into focus.

"I'm outside a train station," Colleen whispered. "No, a . . . a subway station."

"Where are you?" Roni's voice asked.

"I don't know. Wait. Someone's coming toward me I'll ask."

A well-dressed, dapper-looking older gentleman wearing a bowler hat and carrying an umbrella was walking on the sidewalk toward Colleen.

"Excuse me, sir," Colleen asked him. "But can you tell me where I am?"

The gentleman tipped his hat. "Certainly, miss," he said with a British accent. "This is Charing Cross station."

"You're British!" Colleen exclaimed. "Am I in London?"

"Colleen?" Roni asked.

"I'm in London," Colleen whispered.

"Why yes, quite right," the man said. He looked concerned. "See here, miss, if you need help, I can—"

His voice was cut off by the sound of sirens wailing.

"Oh, curse them and their blasted air raids," he commented on the sirens. "At least we're near a shelter."

"Air raid?" Colleen asked, confused and frightened by the foreboding wailing.

The man respectfully took Colleen's arm. "Come along, then, miss," he said. "You seem a bit confused. Or is it just stiff upper lip and all that?"

"I am confused," Colleen admitted.

"You're safe, Colleen," she could hear Roni say.

"But I don't feel safe," Colleen said.

"Who would, with the bloody Nazis bombing London again," the man said. "Let's get you to the shelter, young miss."

"The Nazis?" Colleen whispered hoarsely. "What year is this?"

But the man didn't answer. In any case, the sirens were too loud for Colleen to be heard as the man hurriedly led her downstairs into the subway station and the first wave of German bombers droned overhead.

four
♪

For several minutes in the shelter, Colleen wavered be-
tween two worlds—the modern world she had left
behind and the world of London she was now inhab-
iting. It was like she was two people, with two his-
tories, co-existing in one girl's body.

Then shock waves from a nearby explosion rum-
bled through the shelter. Colleen shivered with fear
as the subway station shook and dust fell from the
ceiling. Somewhere close, she knew, there was death
and devastation.

When the rumbling stopped and the dust settled,
she looked around at her fellow Britains. They were
okay. She was okay. She was surviving the attack.
And she was no longer Colleen Belmont.

In fact, Colleen had never heard of Colleen Belmont, for Colleen Belmont did not exist. Colleen
Belmont had not yet been born; she would not be born
for decades to come.

Colleen was, instead, Colleen Wellington, a girl
celebrating her eighteenth birthday that very day. She
lived in a flat with her parents in the Chelsea section
of London. The year was 1940. Her father was a pilot
with the Royal Air Force and flew Spitfire fighter

planes. Her mother ran a small clothing shop. Colleen was a nursing student at the Royal Victoria Hospital.

Ever since she was a little girl, she'd been in love with the boy next door, Karl Parsons, and he with her. She'd kissed him for the first time when they were both six, and he'd rescued her adored pet rabbit from a mean boy on the playground. And ever since, every time she had a pet rabbit that died or ran away, Karl always gave her a new one.

Everyone had always known that Colleen and Karl would marry one day. And this past year, with Colleen in nursing school and Karl apprenticing to a master carpenter, they'd begun shyly to discuss it.

But that was before she'd met Lawrence Fackler.

She'd heard of Lawrence, of course. Everyone had. At age twenty, he was a violin virtuoso and the toast of London. Until recently a poor, albeit incredibly talented unknown, he had become famous for setting up his violin and music stand on street corners during the daily Nazi air raids, seemingly to taunt the Nazi pilots with his incredible music.

Almost overnight, Lawrence became a hero. He caught the imagination of the British people and lifted their spirits. There had been many newspaper stories about him, his music, and his bravery. He had even been interviewed on the BBC radio. He was a symbol of resolve for Britain—no bomb could touch him.

It had been only by chance that she'd met him one afternoon in Hyde Park. She'd been walking home from her nursing classes, and he'd been playing his violin for an enthralled crowd of admirers. She'd stood on the outskirts of the crowd, taking in the beauty that was Lawrence—drop-dead handsome, with thick blond hair, piercing blue eyes, and the broad shoulders of a Hollywood movie star.

Not to mention his music.

It had been a dark day, and suddenly the skies opened up. People ran for cover, and without thinking about it, Colleen pulled out her umbrella and held it over Lawrence and his violin. As she stood there getting soaked herself, she kept him and his precious violin dry.

They'd gone for tea after that, and she'd been so excited she could barely speak. When he asked to see her again, she could only nod. Wait until she told her mum, and all her friends, that she had a date with Lawrence Fackler!

That was the beginning, and they'd been seeing each other ever since. It had been hard to break up with Karl, but surely it was better for both of them in the long run. After all, they were only still together out of habit. Neither of them had ever dated anyone else. She would love him forever, she'd told him. As a dear friend.

When Karl replied that he would love her forever, *period*, something inside her heart caught for a moment. But the moment didn't last. She wouldn't let it.

She was Lawrence Fackler's girlfriend. Even now, after months of dating, she still wondered what he saw in her. She came from a decidedly unposh section of London. Her family was ordinary and middle-class. And though people said she was pretty, with her long red hair and her flashing blue eyes, she wasn't exactly Betty Grable. And Lawrence Fackler could get any girl in London. He was gorgeous, talented, and a brave hero.

Actually, Colleen knew Lawrence wasn't all that heroic. In fact, he was rather apolitical. He had an ulterior motive for what he was doing. It seemed to her that recently Lawrence had an ulterior motive for everything.

"Look at the publicity it gets me, Colleen," he'd tell her. "I'm the toast of London now, instead of just another struggling musician."

"But you're risking your life!" she'd say.

"I look quite dashing while doing it, don't I?" he'd tease. "Anyway, when it's time for one to go, it's time for one to go. Meanwhile, I'm becoming quite the star."

"Your talent would have made you a star anyway," she'd always tell him. And he'd beam at her with love.

Love. Was it love? He never actually said the words. But he took her everywhere with him, to all the most exciting parties and soirees of the rich and famous, places she never, ever would have been invited on her own. Her mum was forever scrambling to add a lace collar to a dress, or to sew on a bit of velvet, so that Colleen would look as if she had more of a wardrobe than she actually had.

Recently, Colleen had accompanied Lawrence to a party at the American Embassy, where he'd performed to a standing ovation. And the few other young girls there had all whispered to her how lucky she was to be his girlfriend.

"There's a rumor going 'round that I'm to be invited to play at Buckingham Palace," he'd told her recently while kissing her neck. "You'd love to meet the king, wouldn't you? And Churchill?"

Of course she would. And his kisses made her weak and breathless. Still, she wished there was some way that she could get him to stop taking the crazy risks he did. And she felt guilty that he didn't care about the war, but only about how to use it to his own advantage.

Unlike Karl, who was in the army now. She'd gotten a letter from him recently, with most of it blacked out by the censors. One part they hadn't blacked out said that he carried her picture with him, next to his heart.

Sometimes she wondered whether Lawrence loved his career more than he loved her. She'd timidly asked him once. "There's a war on, my love," he'd told her. "It's a nasty business, full of death and dying and deceit and decay. Let's live in the moment and be gay and passionate and young—there isn't anything else." Then he'd kissed her so hard that she'd forgotten about everything.

Lawrence was right about part of what he said. There was a war on. The Netherlands, Belgium, Luxembourg—all had been taken practically overnight in the Nazi onslaught. Then, Britain's ally France had fallen in a matter of weeks.

Now, Radio Berlin was warning in its English-language broadcasts that Britain was the next target of Hitler's wrath. The British ought to surrender now, the radio blared. Otherwise, the river Thames would run red with English blood.

Winston Churchill, the British prime minister, exhorted his countrymen to hold on. Colleen and her parents listened to him on the radio every night. But the Nazi air assault was fierce, and much of London was already in ruins.

Now, as she hurried home after the all-clear signal, she couldn't get Lawrence out of her mind. It almost seemed as if she was having doubts about her feelings for him. But how could that be? She loved him! She did!

But just lately, after the parties with the famous people and the fine food . . . he'd been pressing her to make love with him. She'd always loved his passionate kisses, but she wasn't ready for more. Her refusals to make love were clearly beginning to irritate him. He accused her of acting like a child. And he reminded her of all the other girls who would be more than willing—thrilled, even—to share the bed of the famous Lawrence Fackler.

Well, if he truly loves me he'll respect my wishes, she thought firmly as she rounded the corner of her block. *And no amount of cajoling or charm will change my mind.* She strode up the street toward her parents' flat, saying a little prayer of thanks that it hadn't been damaged in the latest attack.

To her surprise, Lawrence was waiting for her on the front stoop of her home. He stood up to hug her when she approached. Her breath caught, just as it had the first time she'd seen him.

"Hello, love," he said, holding her close. As always, it felt thrilling. It would be so easy to give in to passion. And she didn't want to lose him. She'd *die* if she lost him.

But that wasn't a reason to compromise her morals, was it? Passion wasn't love, was it?

"What a surprise!" She gazed up at his handsome face.

"Rehearsal ended a bit early, so I thought I'd pop over," he said. "The reed players get so frenetic every time an alert sounds that they speed up all the tempos. Better to stop than to ring their nervous Nellie necks, I say." He smiled into her eyes. "Besides, love, it's your birthday, after all. Did you think I'd forgotten?"

She flushed with happiness that he'd remembered. "Well, you've been so busy lately—"

"Never too busy to remember your birthday, love," he said warmly. "Would you invite me in for a spot of tea?" He held up his violin, nestled safely inside its case. "I can serenade the birthday girl."

Colleen hesitated. Her mother wasn't there—she was busy minding the store. Her father was sleeping these days at his air base near Bristol. And though her mum liked Lawrence a lot, as did her dad, she knew that they would be aghast at the idea of her being alone with him in their flat, no matter how famous he was.

It simply was not done.

Lawrence grinned. "Worried about your mum and dad, then? I promise to be the soul of propriety with their precious daughter. After all, she's precious to me, too."

When he said things like that, she melted. He was so charming. And so devastatingly handsome. And out of all the girls in London, he had chosen her.

"All right," she said impulsively, fitting her key into the lock. "But only for tea, mind."

"Tea it shall be," he agreed easily.

I adore him, she thought. *How could I have ever doubted my feelings for him? Maybe he has a birthday present for me in his pocket. Something personal and thoughtful that shows how well he knows me.*

Colleen led Lawrence into the kitchen. She went to the stove, lit it, and put the teapot on. Lawrence sat down at the kitchen table.

"You look very cozy, bustling around in here," Lawrence commented in a teasing voice.

She smiled, and opened the cupboard, hoping to find something to offer Lawrence with his tea. There were four biscuits in the bottom of the tin. She put them on the table. "I know it's freezing in here," she apologized. "No one can get coal. Keep your coat on. I sleep in mine."

"What do you wear under it? Anything?" he asked.

"Lawrence!" She reached out for the teacups. "We had the most interesting lecture today, on emergency care of people injured by flying shrapnel. The doctor told us that—"

"That's much too dreary to talk about," Lawrence interrupted. He smiled at her. "When is your mum getting home?"

She took two teacups from the cupboard. "Regular time. Around dark."

"Then time is on our side."

Her heart sped up. She kept her back to him, busying herself with the tea things. "For what?"

"For a wonderful birthday celebration for you."

"What do you have in mind?" Colleen asked cautiously.

"A celebration of love," he said softly.

Does that mean he loves me? she wondered. She couldn't look at him.

"I want to make love to you, Colleen," he said.

She blushed. "I told you before, Lawrence, I'm—"

"Not ready," he filled in. "But yesterday you were only seventeen, love. A mere child. Today is your eighteenth birthday. And now, sweet Colleen, you are a woman."

His words sent shivers of desire down her spine. She kept her back to him so he wouldn't see how flustered he'd made her. When the kettle whistled, she fixed their tea, hoping to compose herself before she turned to him.

That's when he began to play. She turned around. Lawrence—handsome, dashing, talented, famous Lawrence—had his violin tucked under his chin. His eyes were closed as he played for her, a birthday concert for one. She leaned against the kitchen counter, and she, too, closed her eyes and let the lush, romantic music fill her.

The last note rang out. Finally, Colleen opened her eyes again. "Oh, Lawrence . . ."

He smiled at her. "Dedicated to you, my love." He carefully put his violin away. "Your birthday present."

For a moment, disappointment filled her, but she shoved it away. "Thank you. That was exquisite."

"As are you. And now, I'd like to prove to you how beautiful I think you are." He took a step toward her.

"But—b-but the tea," she stammered.

"Ah, yes. The tea. Well, then." He looked amused and sat back down.

Relieved, she brought their teacups to the table and sat down, too. That's when she noticed the letter on the table. From Karl. Her mum must have brought in the mail when she'd come home to eat at midday.

"Love letter from a soldier?" Lawrence asked when Colleen picked up the letter.

"From an old friend." She knew it was rude to open it now, but something made her do it anyway. She quickly read the parts that were untouched by the censors.

"I hope this reaches you in time for your birthday . . . only wish I could give you everything you deserve . . . for now I can only give you this." He'd drawn a picture of a bunny.

Tears came to Colleen's eyes.

Lawrence took a sip. He hadn't even noticed that she was upset. "Sometimes I wonder if you appreciate me, Colleen," he mused. "I really do."

She tucked the letter into her pocket. "Oh, but I do, Lawrence. How can you say that?"

"Because of how you treat me," he said sadly. "Are you really so cold?"

She cast her eyes down at her teacup. "You know I'm not cold."

"Do I? Is it so easy to keep yourself out of my arms, Colleen?" He put his hands around the teacup in order to warm them a bit.

"No," she said honestly. "But we aren't married."

"Ah, Colleen, I'm disappointed in you." He took another sip of his tea. "Don't you see the folly of such working-class constrictions in the middle of this war?"

She shook her head. "I don't know. It's how I was raised. It's . . . it's what I believe is right."

He smiled, but something about his eyes looked mean. "You really are so conventional, aren't you? I've found it rather quaint all these months. But truly, dearest, it's growing thin."

She didn't know what to say.

He reached for her hand. "Love finds a way, Colleen. And you do love me. Don't you?"

No.

She was shocked when the answer sprang into her mind. And yet, suddenly, she feared it was true. Lawrence Fackler was by far the most wonderful man she would ever get, she knew that. He had rescued her from an ordinary life. How could she not love him?

He never listens to you.

Why should he, when what he has to say is so much more interesting?

He didn't even bring you a birthday present.

His playing was his gift.

He doesn't love you.

He does!

No. He loves how much you adore him because of how much he adores himself.

"Colleen," he said huskily. He got to his feet and reached for her, pulling her from her chair. He gazed into her eyes. "You love this, don't you?"

He put his right hand behind her head and drew her to him. He kissed her. It was fantastic, all heat and excitement that melted her.

But it wasn't enough. It wasn't love. She knew that now. It was as if someone had just taken her blinders off.

He kissed her. Her mind stopped working and her body took over. It was just so thrilling to be in his arms. But she had to talk to him. Maybe if they had an honest conversation, they could—

"Lawrence, I—"

Her sentence was interrupted by the wail of the air raid sirens.

"Bloody hell," Lawrence cursed.

"The closest tube station is at Sarratt Road. We can be there in two minutes. If we hurry."

"We could stay here," Lawrence said softly, kissing her neck in that way that drove her crazy. "Your mum's definitely not coming home now."

She forced herself to pull away, and shook her head no. "We'd better get out. We're safer down in the shelter."

"But I'm Lawrence Fackler," he said, grinning. "Haven't you read the papers? Nothing can happen to me. I have my magic violin."

As if to mock the Nazis, Lawrence took his violin out of the case again and started to play the second movement funeral march from Beethoven's third symphony, the *Eroica*.

The air raid sirens grew louder.

"Lawrence . . ."

He played on.

She'd lived through many Nazi air attacks, and her dad swore she had a sixth sense about them. She often seemed to feel in advance when the bombs were going to be landing in the city of London or whether the Nazi bombers were headed elsewhere.

She got a terrible feeling.

"Lawrence, come on," she insisted. "It's too dangerous to stay here!"

He stopped playing, finally.

"Please, let's go."

He carefully put his violin on the table. "Do you know your eyes get all fiery when you're aroused?"

"I'm frightened, not . . . the other," she insisted.

"Your body can't tell the difference," he said. Slowly he took off his coat. Then he unbuttoned the top button of his shirt.

"Lawrence!"

He undid another button.

"Lawrence—"

He completely unbuttoned his shirt, and stood there with an extremely goofy expression on his face. He held out his arms. "Come to me, Colleen."

Poof. In less than an instant, all her desire for him was gone. He was just an egocentric, self-involved idiot, albeit an extremely talented one.

And she had never before noticed how utterly goofy he could look.

An odd whistle filled the air, one that neither had heard before. Outside.

It was coming from above.

Colleen knew. She couldn't move, couldn't scream. All she could do was stand there and wonder how she could have been so silly, so insecure and needy, as to have stayed with Lawrence all these months.

And one word sprang to her lips. *Karl.*

But she never got to say it. The flat was obliterated by a Nazi bomb dropped by a dive-bomber that had eluded the British antiaircraft fire and fighter planes.

She died with Karl's name on her lips and his drawing of a bunny in her pocket. The last thing she saw was Lawrence, a ridiculous fellow she didn't really love, with his shirt unbuttoned. He had the most idiotic expression on his face.

five

Monday, at the flagpole in front of school, Kevin kissed Colleen good-bye before he went to swim practice.

"I'll call you later," he promised. Then he shivered. "Geez, it's freezing. Thank God for indoor pools."

"Get going, or you'll be frozen here forever and you won't be able to kiss me again until you thaw out in the spring."

He smiled at her. "It's good to see you back to normal. You were pretty weirded out yesterday, you have to admit." She'd called him Saturday night, and had told him exactly what had happened during her past life regression.

"It's not every day you find out that you died in a previous life when a Nazi bomb incinerates your house."

"Come on, Colleen, you can't really believe that."

The bitter wind off Lake Michigan whipped her hair into her face, and she pushed it away. "I don't know if I believe it or not. It might be true. It felt so real, Kevin—"

"You were hypnotized into believing it, that's all," he insisted. "You've seen war movies, read books about it, and you are a girl with a vivid imagination.''

''So you keep saying.'' Colleen sighed. She looked off into the distance. How could she know what was real? How could anyone?

''Let's just forget about it, okay?'' Kevin suggested. He looked at his watch. ''I gotta run, or Coach is gonna drop me onto the diving board headfirst.''

''And I have to go to the computer lab and reformat my movie review. Tolliver does these things just to torture me.''

When Colleen had arrived at school that morning, there was a memo in her box in the newspaper office from Tolliver. He had mandated a complicated new format for all articles coming into the *Lakesider*. The memo said that if articles were not submitted in the new format, there would be no chance of their appearing in the paper.

''Hey, one day you'll be a rich and famous film critic and he'll still be picking out weenie bow ties,'' Kevin said, hugging her quickly. ''I'll call you later.''

She hurried back into the building, heading for the computer lab. It was bad enough that she'd had to sit through and write a review of a truly awful movie starring Pamela Anderson. Now she had to spend even more time reformatting the stupid review. What a waste of time.

She turned down the hall that led to the computer lab, and glanced down at her own chest, which was clearly not surgically enhanced.

Fine by me, Colleen thought. *Who would pay to have someone slice them open and stick silicon baggies in their chest and then pay again to have them removed? Now, that's way creepier than past life regression.*

That thought made her laugh aloud. Which was good, because she'd been kind of brooding and pre-occupied since her regression experience.

"You look happy," a voice said.

A voice she knew. Low, sexy, just slightly Southern. Luke Ransom fell into step beside her. He wore black jeans and a black sweater, which looked great below his blond hair.

"Hi," she said, hoping to sound much more casual than she felt. Just being near him made her feel flustered.

"Where are you heading?"

"Computer lab," Colleen said. "I've got to reformat the review I wrote."

"Movie review, I take it," Luke said.

"Yes, how did you know?" Colleen asked him.

Luke stopped, and Colleen automatically stopped, too. Then his piercing blue eyes were looking deeply into hers. "I can read your mind," he told her.

Her mouth fell open.

He laughed. "I read the *Lakesider,* that's how I know. Your byline is above your reviews. "Great paper. I especially love Tolliver's editorials. So . . . penetrating in their analysis. What a suck-up."

The two of them looked at each other for a moment longer before they burst out laughing.

"Well . . ." Colleen smiled as they headed down the hall again. "I hope you're not a big fan of Pamela Anderson's. You might be disappointed in what I wrote about her."

Luke got a shocked look on his face. "But she's the greatest living American actress."

Colleen nodded seriously. "You know, you're right. I admit it. I only panned her performance because I'm seething with jealousy over her, shall we say, *unnatural* abilities.''

"Hey, she had reversal surgery. I suppose she felt you *can* have too much of a good thing," Luke said. "It's sort of bizarre.''

"It's very bizarre," Colleen agreed.

"A natural woman is so much more beautiful than all that cartoon stuff. I mean, look at you.''

She took a step backward. "Oh, well . . .''

He laughed. "You know, for a girl who is great with words, you seem at a loss for them every now and then.''

"Because I'm—I'm busy thinking great thoughts," she invented. They were standing just outside the computer lab. "Well, I really have to get in there.''

"You're not wearing a cameo pin today," he noted.

She looked down at her sweater. Today she wore a malachite pin shaped like a butterfly. It had been a present from Kevin last Valentine's Day.

"I like cameos better," Luke said. Then he gave her a strange wave, like cutting the air with a little karate chop straight down, and then making a sharp right angle with his palm down.

Colleen recognized the unique wave. It was from one of her favorite old movies of all time, *Giant*. James Dean had played a poor guy named Jett Rink who was in love with rich Elizabeth Taylor. One day, he struck it rich at a big oil well.

That was the Jett Rink wave. I'm sure of it.

She couldn't resist trying a line from the movie out on Luke, to see if he knew what he had just done. If he didn't, what she was about to say would make absolutely no sense at all.

"Did your well come in, Luke?''

His eyes lit up. "It came in big, so big," Luke quoted Jett. "I'm a rich 'un."

"You know *Giant*," she said.

"I love *Giant*," Luke told her.

It thrilled her. And scared her, too.

"I've got to go to work," she said quickly. "It was nice talking to you. See ya."

She turned away from him.

"Colleen."

She turned back.

"Wear the cameo," he said. And then he walked away.

Colleen stared at what she'd just written on the computer screen. It wasn't her review. It was as if a force within her had made her write these words, instead of reformatting her review of *Platinum Danger*.

It was 1940. I was a girl named Colleen Wellington and it was my birthday. I was not American, but British. I lived in London. I had always lived in the city of London. I had a boyfriend named Lawrence who played the violin. He was famous and exciting. After I met him, I broke up with Karl, the boy who had loved me since grammar school. But Karl couldn't compete with dashing Lawrence. It was the Nazi blitz, and the Nazis were bombing London.

I was turning eighteen that very day. There were air raid sirens. I tried to get Lawrence to go to the shelter. He wouldn't go. All he cared about was himself. That was when I finally admitted to myself that I didn't really love him. I had only been dazzled by him, and flattered that he wanted me. But I hid the truth from myself for so long that I was there, with him, at my flat. That's when the Nazi dive-bombers attacked, and it was too late. Our home was destroyed and I died. The last thing I remember was him unbuttoning his shirt.

This is what happened to me when I went back in time in my mind. Is it real? Is anything real? It felt as real as my life does now. So I ask you, what does it all mean?

I don't know, but I'm going to find out. I'm going to do it again. I swear it.

"Hi."

Colleen was so startled that she literally jumped a little in her seat before she whirled around to see who was behind her.

Luke.

Has he seen what I just wrote?

Colleen spun back around and quickly closed down her document, even before she said a word to him. Only after she was back on the main menu of her word-processing program did she turn again to him.

"What are you doing here?" she asked him.

"Reading over your shoulder," he admitted. "I wanted to read your review. But I don't think that was it."

Colleen stood up and faced him. "I don't like people reading over my shoulder. Especially people I never invited to read what I wrote in the first place."

A few other kids in the computer lab turned to look at her, so she lowered her voice.

"What I was writing up there was private," she said.

Luke looked directly into her eyes. "I understand."

"Well, if you understand, why did you do it?"

"No, I mean . . ." He turned away from her and ran his hand through his hair, then he turned back. "Look, I wasn't planning to come back here to you."

She folded her arms. "Then, why did you?"

"Shhh!" a girl a few computers down hissed at them. "Some people are trying to work in here."

Luke cocked his head toward the hall, then walked out the door into the corridor. Colleen stood there fuming for a minute, then she followed him.

"I don't usually follow girls into computer labs and read their stuff," Luke said, his voice low. "Some force just told me to do it."

"Is this some kind of a joke?" Colleen asked.

"No, it's—"

"Hi, Luke," April Sommersby said as she walked by. She had a huge crush on him and had been trying to get him to notice her ever since he'd shown up at Lakeside.

"Hi," Luke said tersely, his eyes on Colleen.

"Oh, hi, Colleen," April added. "Does Kevin know you guys are out here?"

Colleen made a noise of exasperation. Luke touched her elbow lightly, then headed across the hall into the auditorium. She followed him.

The auditorium was empty, except for the two of them, the stage bare save for the seats and music stands of the Lakeside school orchestra that usually practiced in there.

Luke leaned against the back row of seats. "Better."

Colleen looked at her watch. "Five minutes, that's it, then I'm getting back to work."

Luke nodded. "What I was trying to say is this. I felt compelled, deeply compelled, to come back to see you. To read what you wrote. And I've learned that when I get that feeling, I should listen to it."

"What, so that's supposed to make it okay?" Colleen asked.

"I told you before that you could talk to me about the stuff you want to write for the paper. I would understand."

She looked at him warily. "So?"

"So, I *do* understand."

"Right. And I suppose you're going to tell me that you've done past life regressions yourself."

Those eyes pulled Colleen's gaze toward them again. They locked. Her knees went liquid.

"Does the name Raymond Moody mean anything to you?"

"Who's he?" Colleen bluffed.

"You know who he is," Luke insisted. "He wrote the book on regression experiences through hypnosis. How about Brian Weiss? He came up with the concept. He's the licensed psychiatrist who found regression by accident. You should read his books, too."

Colleen went to the seats and sat in the back row. This was all just too intense. She was feeling so many things. Including confused.

Luke sat next to her. "You did a regression, didn't you?"

She shook her head yes.

"How was it?"

"Weird. Very weird. Extremely weird."

"Want to talk about it?"

Yes, every fiber of her being told her to say. *I desperately, desperately want to talk about it with you. I want to tell you everything that happened, from start to finish.*

"No," Colleen replied. She couldn't look at him.

"You sure?"

She nodded yes.

"When you're ready . . ." Luke said to her. "And I'll tell you about some of my own."

Now she did turn to him. "You've done it, too? Really?"

"You can't be what you haven't done," Luke said. "And you can't know who you are unless you know who you've been. Fear of knowing holds people back. People just need to open their minds."

"I wish Kevin felt that way." She clapped her hand over her mouth, instantly sorry she'd blurted out the truth.

"Kevin," Luke said. "The guy whose ring you're not wearing."

"Look, forget I even mentioned him, okay?" Colleen said quickly. She felt guilty and disloyal. "I don't want to talk about him."

"Good. I don't, either."

He moved closer to her. An inch. Two inches.

She gulped. Her heart quickened. Was he going to kiss her, right here and now?

And if he did, what would she do?

Stop him, pull away, move right now, she told herself. But his eyes held hers, and she could no more move or protest than she could stop breathing.

His lips were so close now. So close. So—

She never heard the auditorium door open.

"Colleen!" a familiar voice called from behind them. "What are you doing in here?"

six

*B*etsy took a sip of her hot chocolate and peered over the cup at her best friend. Colleen's own hot chocolate cup sat in front of her untouched, the steam curling the fine, red hair by her ears. She stared into the distance, utterly lost in thought.

"Colleen?" Betsy said.

No answer.

"Uh, Earth to Colleen?" Betsy said, speaking a little louder. "Would you mind returning to charming, sweet, and extremely boring Wisconsin for a few minutes so your nearest and dearest friend can bust your chops?"

Colleen focused on Betsy. "Sorry. I was thinking."

"Big duh on that one, Belmont."

Colleen just shrugged.

The two of them were seated at one of the wooden tables scattered around the Edmund Fitz, a coffee-house on Lakeside's main drag, oh-so-imaginatively called Main Street. The Edmund Fitz was as close as Lakeside, Wisconsin, came to a hip place to hang out. It was named after the *Edmund Fitzgerald*, a big ship that had gone down on Lake Michigan many years before when the winds of November had come early.

"All I have to say is, be glad it was me and not Kevin who walked into the auditorium," Betsy said, "because if Kevin saw you alone in there with Sugar Lips Luke, he'd give birth."

"Colorfully put," Colleen said.

"I thought so. Correct me if my perfect vision was deceiving me, but it looked as if Sugar Lips was about to kiss you."

"That's crazy."

"Uh huh. And it also looked like you wanted him to."

"I didn't," Colleen insisted. "I don't."

Betsy eyed her skeptically. "Yo, girlfriend. This is Betsy Wu you're lying to."

Colleen put her head down on her hands and groaned. "Okay. You're right. God, Bets, I can't believe what almost happened."

"I can. Luke is walking fine."

"So? I'm not some stupid little twit who goes all breathy because a cute guy crooks his finger at me!" Colleen exclaimed. "And Kevin is cute, too. And I love him."

Betsy smiled. "Set it to music and bring in the fiddles. You might have a future in Nashville."

"Would you please get serious?" Colleen asked.

"Okay, consider me serious. You should seriously send flowers to April Sommersby for telling me that she saw you and Sugar Lips go into the auditorium together."

"Stop calling him that."

Betsy wriggled her eyebrows. "How about Luscious Lips, then?"

"Betsy, you are not being what I would call helpful."

"True," Betsy agreed. "But I am being what you would call entertaining." She saw the real distress etched on Colleen's face. "Okay, joke's over," she assured her friend. "Really. I'm glad I saved you."

Colleen puffed out her lower lip and blew air over it. "Me, too."

It had been almost funny. Betsy standing there; Luke turning to her with that easy smile of his and asking her what he could do for her. When Betsy had said to Colleen that her mom was waiting outside for them both, Luke had just nodded easily. Then he'd given her the swiftest of special looks, said so long, and loped out of the auditorium.

"You know, Luke is one of those guys who looks good coming and going," Betsy decided. "It's fun to walk toward him and fun to walk behind—"

"Betsy," Colleen chided her.

"Yeah, I know, be serious. But can I help it if I'm testosterone-deprived since I broke up with Brandon?"

Betsy and Brandon Marrow, the arts writer for the *Lakesider*, had broken up a month earlier when Betsy had caught Brandon out with some cheerleader who went to Brown Deer High School.

"You're too good for Brandon, and everyone knows it," Colleen told her. She shook her head ruefully. "You know how the Lakeside rumor mill is. If it had been anyone but you who had walked into the auditorium, by eight o'clock tonight somebody would be calling Kevin to tell him that Luke and I were going at it on top of the grand piano in the orchestra pit."

"We could sell videos of that and make a mint," Betsy mused.

"That is so not funny, Wu."

"It's terrible when you're your own best audience," Betsy said. "Okay. Tell me. What's really up with you two?"

"Nothing."

"Nice try," Betsy said.

Colleen stared out the picture window. It was already dark out—in December, night fell early. "Okay. I admit that I'm attracted to him, but . . . people get attracted to people all the time, don't they? I mean, your mom might be attracted to someone besides your father, right?"

Betsy made a face and shuddered. "Please do not allude to anything remotely connected to sex in the same breath that you mention my parents."

"You know what I mean. Attraction is just . . . hormones. It doesn't mean anything."

"The Wreck of the Edmund Fitzgerald," the ballad by Gordon Lightfoot about the sinking of the ship, came over the sound system. It got played in the Edmund Fitz once a day. All desserts purchased while the song was playing were half price, provided you sang along to the cashier.

"You want to split a brownie?" Betsy asked her friend. "I'll humiliate myself and sing a verse to save a buck and a half."

Colleen shook her head.

"Well, that little tune certainly matches your gloomy mood," Betsy noted. "Are you, like, so-o-o-o sorry and all that?"

Colleen knew she should be. She had almost cheated on Kevin. But the truth was, although she felt guilty, she didn't feel sorry. And not feeling sorry

59

made her feel even more guilty. What she felt was energized somehow. Like Luke had some sort of strange power over her.

And she liked it.

But she loved Kevin. Loved him. And she wasn't the type to cheat.

"Luke is just—well, he's different," Colleen said. "I don't know how to explain it."

"Give it a whirl," Betsy suggested.

Colleen took another sip of her hot chocolate. "There are things I care about that Luke cares about. That Kevin doesn't care about."

"Such as?"

"Past life regression, for one thing."

"No kidding? Huh." Betsy put her feet up on the chair and drew her knees to her chest. "So, this is how Dr. Wu sees it. Luscious Lips is into the Unified Belmont Theory of Ultimate Cosmic Forces, and Bodacious Boyfriend is not. Because of this, Beleaguered Belmont feels a common bond with Luscious Lips that feels stronger than current bond with Bodacious Boyfriend. But what kind of bond is it, really? The bouncing ball is now in Belmont's court, and you'll find my bill in the mail."

"He's done regressions, Bets."

Betsy leaned forward, her voice serious. "Really?"

Colleen nodded. "Lots of them, I think. He's so intense about it. And you know how Kevin just blows it all off. I can't talk to him about it without getting lectured on how ridiculous it all is."

Betsy nodded her agreement.

Colleen drummed her fingers on the table. "I've been thinking. Betsy, I want to do another regression."

The music changed to something by Barenaked Ladies, and Betsy started to bop to the beat. "I love this song. No can do, Colleen. Roni is back in Chicago and won't be home until Christmas."

"You can do it," Colleen said.

Betsy snorted back a laugh. "Yeah, right. I'm not trained."

"You don't need to be," Colleen insisted. "You were there during my regression; you saw exactly what Roni did."

"I've seen them do surgery on *ER*, too, but that doesn't mean I'd take out your appendix," Betsy said.

"It's not like that. Look, there's even a script for regressions in the back of Moody's book."

She opened her backpack, pulled out her dog-eared copy of *Coming Back*, and flipped it open to the back. "See? Right here." She thrust the book at Betsy.

"Forget it." Betsy pushed the book back at Colleen.

"But—"

"This isn't stuff to fool around with, Colleen."

Colleen leaned closer to her friend. "I'm not fooling around. I'm as serious as I've ever been about anything in my life."

"I don't know. . . ."

Colleen could see that Betsy was wavering. "We can do it this weekend," she went on. "Kat's in a tennis tournament in Madison; it's, like, the Wisconsin Christmas Invitational or something. Everyone will be away. Please?"

Betsy thought for a moment. "I don't suppose I could do anything too awful."

"Of course you couldn't," Colleen agreed. "I trust you completely."

"We'd follow Moody's script exactly," Betsy insisted.

"Absolutely," Colleen agreed.

"And I have to call Roni first and make sure it's cool."

"Agreed," Colleen said eagerly. "So? Will you do it?"

Betsy sighed. "Why do I let you talk me into these things?"

Colleen jumped up and hugged Betsy across the table. "I love you, Betsy Wu. I knew I could count on you. You won't be sorry."

Betsy extricated herself from Colleen's embrace and threw her balled-up napkin at her friend. "I'm sorry already."

"Hi," Kevin said as he came up to Colleen at her locker. He was carrying a copy of the new issue of the *Lakesider*. It had just come out that day.

"Hi, there," Colleen said, standing on tiptoe to kiss him lightly. She was in a great mood. She'd gotten through the rest of the week without even running into Luke. Her parents and sister were going to be away until Sunday night. And Betsy was going to do a past life regression with her on Saturday afternoon.

"So," Colleen went on, "my parents will be in Madison for the whole weekend watching Kat humiliate everyone else in her age bracket. She's seeded first, of course. Are you planning to come over to take advantage of the situation?"

Kevin smiled, but the smile never reached his eyes.

"I take it that's a yes?" Colleen asked.

Kevin didn't say anything.

She got a terrible feeling in the pit of her stomach.

"What's wrong?" she asked him. "Is someone sick or something?"

"Have you seen the *Lakesider* yet?"

A hot flush came to Colleen's cheeks. "Tolliver cut my review? I knew it. He's dog meat in a bow tie. Well, I've had it. He's going to hear exactly what I think about his—"

"It's not Tolliver, Colleen." Kevin's jaw set tightly.

"Well, what, then? Something bad, I can tell."

"It's Celeste," Kevin said.

Colleen shook her head in confusion. Celeste Durkey, better known as the Curls because of her bouncy blond hair, was an incredibly annoying girl who wrote a gossip column for the *Lakesider.* Actually, her name was Celeste Nan Durkey. Her identical twin sister, Celeste Ann Durkey, had died the previous year when she'd dropped an electric hair dryer into a full bathtub. Unfortunately, she'd been in the bathtub at the time.

"Celeste, as in the Curls?" Colleen asked. "What does she have to do with anything?"

"I guess you haven't seen her column in today's paper," Kevin said. He handed it to her.

She scanned it quickly. The headline on the piece was AFTER HOURS SECRET ROMANCE.

Recently an eyewitness saw C.B. and hottie newcomer L.R. leave the computer lab and head across the hall into an empty auditorium. According to my source, it was *way* after school was out, and they were in there a *way* long time, and when L.R. finally came out, he was wearing C.B.'s lipstick. Wonder if K.A. has heard about this yet. Looks like C.B. is going to have some explaining to do!

Colleen paled. At that moment, she wanted to be anywhere except standing in the hall with Kevin.

"I know the Curls isn't above making stuff up," Kevin said hopefully.

"Right," Colleen agreed, her voice a shade too bright. "She said Tollie asked her to the spring dance already. But that's a lie."

"Just tell me it isn't true, Colleen."

"It isn't true—" Colleen said.

He exhaled loudly. "Oh, man, you don't know how relieved I am—"

"Part of it. And part of it is true." She forced herself to look at him. "I was in the auditorium talking with Luke, that's true. But the other part—the lipstick thing—that's a total lie. Nothing happened."

Kevin's eyebrows rose. "Why didn't you tell me?"

"There was nothing to tell," Colleen said. Her voice felt tight, her palms sweaty.

I should have told him, she said to herself. *Even if nothing happened.*

His eyes searched hers. "You sure?"

"Positive."

He was silent. Then finally he said, "I believe you. You're the most honest girl I know. But I wish you would have told me. To find out like this . . ." He pointed his finger at the school paper she was still holding. "It's kind of humiliating, basically."

"I'm sorry," Colleen said. "Really. And I'd like to immerse Celeste Nan in a full bathtub and drop in an industrial-size air conditioner." She slammed her locker shut. "If there's such a place as Teen Heaven, she would definitely not end up there."

"Colleen, what is with that Luke guy, anyway?"

"What do you mean?"

"You know what I mean." Kevin's voice was intense. "He watches you, Colleen. Don't think I haven't noticed."

"He doesn't watch me—"

"Come on," Kevin insisted. "He watches you all the time. Whenever we're together, Luke shows up. He floats by with those eyes of his, looking at you."

"That's your imagination," Colleen insisted.

"I'm the guy who has no imagination, remember? Mr. Stuck-in-Reality?"

Colleen felt terrible. Kevin sounded so hurt and bitter, and it was her fault. She leaned against her locker and tried to smile at him.

"What were you talking about in the auditorium, anyway?" Kevin asked.

"Nothing. I told you, we—"

Kevin looked at her.

"Okay. If you want to know, we were talking about past life regression. He's interested in it."

"Figures. That's great. Just great." Which, Colleen knew, meant he thought it was anything but okay.

"Can we just forget it?" Colleen asked. "Please?" She reached up to put her arms around his neck.

Kevin looked over her shoulder at the stream of students passing Colleen's locker. Fifty feet away, coming toward them, was Luke Ransom.

"Speak of the devil, here he comes," Kevin complained. "Geez, that guy creeps me out."

Colleen turned around. But Luke wasn't even looking in her direction.

"He's just going to his next class," Colleen said. She reached for Kevin again.

He put his arms around her waist. "Look, next time, if you have a private chat with some new guy, don't let me read about it in the Curls' column, okay?"

"Okay," she agreed. Then she stood on tiptoe again and tenderly kissed him.

Down the hall about thirty yards, Luke Ransom leaned against the bank of lockers and watched them.

And he smiled.

seven
♉

"**A**re you absolutely, positively sure you want to go through with this?" Betsy asked Colleen.

"For the zillionth time, yes." Colleen lay down on her bed. "Let's get started."

It was Saturday afternoon, Christmas was just a few days away, and as Colleen had anticipated, her house was empty. Her parents had called her from Madison an hour before to tell her that Kat had won her first three matches without dropping a set and would be playing in the semifinals that afternoon. If she won—and everyone knew she would—the finals would be Sunday afternoon.

Betsy nervously fingered the script that she and Colleen had written that morning for the past life regression. They'd put it together using some self-hypnosis tapes they'd taken out of the oh-so-imaginatively named Lakeside Public Library, Dr. Moody's book, and some articles they had found on the Internet about hypnosis.

"Maybe we need to work on the script a little more," Betsy suggested.

Colleen sat up. "The script is fine. It's perfect. Anyhow, you can be flexible."

"Colleen—" Betsy began doubtfully.

"I have to do this, Betsy."

"But why?"

"I don't know," Colleen admitted. "I just do." She took Betsy's hand. "It's going to be fine, I promise. Just let me go where I have to go."

Betsy pulled her hand away. "Believe me, Belmont, if I'm not happy about where it looks like you're going, I don't care if you think you have to go there or not. I'm bringing you out of it so fast you'll think it's yesterday."

"I trust you completely," Colleen said serenely, lying back down.

"I wish I did," Betsy mumbled, fingering the script again. She closed her eyes. *Think peaceful thoughts,* she told herself. *Colleen needs all the peace around her she can get. Please don't let me mess this up.*

She got up and dimmed the lights with the dimmer switch. "Better?" she asked.

Colleen nodded. "Don't forget to turn on the tape recorder. I want to hear this later."

"Yeah, fine, whatever." She still didn't feel very peaceful. But she dutifully pressed the record button on Colleen's portable cassette player.

Colleen got comfortable and closed her eyes.

"Your whole body is beginning to relax," Betsy read. "Let all the tension leave your body. You feel safe and relaxed, relaxed and safe."

These were the exact same things Roni had said when she'd regressed Colleen. Betsy hadn't been able to reach her sister to get the go-ahead for this regression, so she'd stuck as closely to what Roni had said and done as possible.

"Your arms and legs are getting heavy. Your whole

body is more and more relaxed. So relaxed," Betsy read.

Colleen quickly found herself drifting off into a twilight state. If anything, her friend Betsy's voice was even more comforting and familiar than Roni's had been.

"You are very rested," Betsy said. "Everything feels heavy."

It did.

"Heavier and heavier," Betsy went on. "More and more relaxed. Now, I'm going to count you back. With each number, you'll be even more rested, more relaxed, more comfortable. Ten . . . nine . . ."

Colleen felt her chest rise and fall slowly. She had the sensation both of floating and of weighing a million tons. It didn't bother her. She felt strangely calm.

Betsy continued counting backward. "Three . . . two . . . one."

Betsy continued, taking Colleen deeper and deeper, to that safe place on the beach with Kevin. And then Colleen was floating up, farther and farther, floating out of the body that was her but wasn't her. The essential *her* was now far, far above the Earth. It felt so natural and peaceful. And then, just as gently, she floated back down to Earth.

This time, she knew where she was even before she opened her eyes.

It was November 1864. She was fifteen miles or so south of Nashville, Tennessee, in a small town called Franklin.

Her name was Colleen Berendt, and she was the daughter of a well-known Tennessee legislator who had once been a congressman in Washington but was now a part of President Jefferson Davis's Confederate legislature. The Union army, tens of thousands of soldiers, was moving north from Spring Hill, Tennessee, poised to deliver a crushing blow to the rebel South. So many young men she knew were soldiers. So many of her friends could die.

And it was, once again, Colleen's eighteenth birthday.

"It's all so sad," Colleen said.

Betsy let out a small gasp. Colleen had just spoken with a Southern accent.

"Tell me what you see," Betsy said.

"Troops," Colleen replied. "As far as you can see, our troops."

"Whose army?"

"The Army of the Confederacy, of course," Colleen said as if Betsy had asked the stupidest question in the world. "Not those horrible Yankees. I curse them all!"

Whoa. Betsy forced her voice to remain calm. "Can you tell me what your name is? What you are doing right now?"

"I'm Colleen Berendt. Everyone knows me, on account of my father bein' in the legislature. I'm walking amongst our troops. There are so many encampments here. Everywhere I look. There are campfires burnin'. Some men are singin' and playin' the harmonica. Their mournful songs go right through me. They're so young and so brave. I know I shouldn't think it, but . . ."

"But what?" Betsy asked her.

"I know how selfish I am," Colleen went on in her soft, Southern twang. "But I keep thinkin' that this is a terrible way for me to celebrate my eighteenth birthday."

Betsy couldn't decide if she felt excited or sick.

Why had Colleen regressed to her eighteenth birthday again, but in a different lifetime?

"Your birthday is special," Betsy ventured, hoping Colleen would give them both some kind of clue.

"Well, of course," Colleen said. "I dreamt about my eighteenth birthday for so long." Her voice was full of longing. "There would have been cotillion balls, and I would have had the most wonderful gowns. I would have piled all my red hair up on my head, and worn Aunt Dru's tiara from her cotillion ball. And I would have danced and flirted with Lyndon and Kingsley and all the other handsome boys. But now . . ."

"Now?" Betsy prompted.

"Now there's just this," Colleen said sadly. "No one can get any material for fancy gowns. We barely have enough food to eat. And all the handsome boys have gone to be soldiers."

"Who are Lyndon and Kingsley?" Betsy asked.

"You know very well who they are," Colleen said, her voice weirdly flirtatious.

"No," Betsy said. "You have to tell me."

"Oh, hush. This is no time for me to talk about my suitors, and you know it."

Colleen looked around at the young soldiers trying to warm their hands at the fires. She wrapped her shawl more tightly around herself, and shivered. A song her momma used to sing to her came into her mind. She closed her eyes and let the song flow from both her lips and heart.

Alberta, let your hair hang low.
Alberta, let your hair hang low.
I'll give you more gold than your

71

pockets will hold.
If you'll only let your hair hang low.

"What's that song?" a familiar voice asked.

Somehow Colleen knew it was Betsy, someone she loved and trusted. "It's a sad song," she said aloud. "A young man would sing it, I think. A young man at war, who is lonely and tired and scared. And he's longin' to see Alberta again, because anything beautiful seems as if it was just a dream he once had."

She began to sing again.

Alberta, what's on your mind?
Alberta, what's on your mind?
Your eyes are like twin pools of fire
in the night.
Alberta, what's on your mind?

Betsy shivered. This was major weird. Not just because Betsy had never heard the song before. And not just because she was almost positive that Colleen didn't know the song, either. What was really weird was that the singing voice coming from Colleen Berendt was melodious, sweet, really lovely.

And Colleen Belmont couldn't sing. In fact, she was a really terrible singer who could barely carry a tune. Every year when they went Christmas caroling, all their friends would tease Colleen about it and tell her to please just mouth the carols so that people wouldn't throw snowballs at them.

Betsy snuck a quick look at the cassette recorder, which was whirring away.

"That was beautiful," Betsy told her.

"Thank you. Do you think I should sing it for the soldiers, or would it make them sadder?"

"Uh, I don't know." Betsy was at a total loss.

"Sometimes I wish I could be a soldier, too," Colleen went on, her voice impassioned. "Why do women stay behind, wringin' their hands, while the men become heroes? It isn't right."

"Men die in wars," Betsy told her.

"I know that. My father says I romanticize things. I suppose he's right."

"Where are you right now?" Betsy asked. "What are you doing?"

Colleen lifted the heavy basket in her nearly frozen hands. "It's so heavy," she said. "Full of potatoes for the boys to cook. I'm takin' it to them. There's a little hardtack in there, too. Awful stuff, hardtack. Have you tasted it?"

"No."

Colleen approached a group of soldiers sitting near a fire. "Fourth Company, Seventh Regiment, Army of Tennessee. It's Lyndon and Kingsley's company. They're fighting under Major General Cleburne."

The boys around the fire nodded politely at Colleen as she put the basket down.

"Thanks, ma'am," one of them said.

"What are they wearing?" Betsy asked.

Colleen looked down at the soldiers' feet. "Their shoes aren't much more than rags on their feet. No shoes for a long time. Blockade at New Orleans cut off the—"

Boom—in the distance.

She stopped talking. She had heard something. The soldiers had heard it, too. They stopped cooking the potatoes. Everyone stood still, listening.

Boom—again, louder this time. *Boom-boom.*

"It's Yankee cannon," Colleen whispered. Her

blood felt cold now. "They're comin' from the south. It's the Yankee artillery, I'm sure.

"Fixin' to give me a birthday present."

Betsy was tense and exhausted. Only a few minutes had passed, but she felt as if she'd been with Colleen Berendt for days. Colleen had narrated her actions for Betsy as she explained that a colonel had told her to please go up to the house with the other women. Colleen had hated that, but she'd complied.

Now, she said she was on the porch of someplace called Carter House, rolling bandages with a dozen or so other women. All over the lawn, for acres and acres, Confederate soldiers huddled around campfires.

Betsy paced as she spoke. "What's happening, Colleen?"

"The Yanks think they can drive us away just by showing their colors," Colleen said vehemently. "Well, I'll tell you, they've got another thing coming."

Specifics, Betsy thought. *I should try to get specifics.*

"What are the names of the women who are with you, Colleen?"

"Let's see, there's Beth Anne, and Susannah, of course—bless her heart, she puts in more time than any of us. And Mrs. Chiles—both her sons are fightin' somewhere out west—she hasn't had a letter in the longest time. And Elenora. She's my dearest friend. This is so hard for her, because her brother is livin' in New York with his—"

Betsy heard Colleen gasp.

"What? What is it, Colleen? Are you okay?"

"My stars, the two of them, together," Colleen said. "I can't believe it."

"Who?" Betsy asked.

"I know, Elenora, I see them, too," Colleen said. Clearly, she wasn't speaking to Betsy. "Lyndon and Kingsley. Someone must have told them I'm here. They're comin' to see me, I know it."

Betsy heard Colleen Berendt give a tinkling laugh that was so totally *not* Colleen Belmont, she shivered.

"Oh, hush, Elenora. I already know they hate each other," Colleen said. "You make jokes at the worst possible times, you really do."

"What jokes?" Betsy asked. "Tell me what she said."

"I can't talk to you anymore right now," Colleen told her, her voice growing faint. "I have to talk to Lyndon and Kingsley."

"You have to talk to me, Colleen," Betsy demanded. "I mean it."

Roni had once told her it was important to keep the regressed subject talking with you, because it was the thread between this world and the regression.

"We'll talk later," Colleen promised. "Lyndon! Kingsley!" she called.

"Wait, Colleen, you have to keep talking to me—"

"I'm just so glad to see you," Colleen went on. Clearly, she wasn't talking to Betsy.

"Colleen!" Betsy looked at her friend, who lay on her bed, a smile on her lips. She didn't know if she should wake Colleen up or not.

"I'm fine, gentl'men, thank you for askin'," Colleen said sweetly. "I'm *fine*. Perfectly safe."

That last part was for me, Betsy thought. *I hope.*

She sat back and waited, every muscle in her body tensed. But if Colleen did or said one thing that was too bizarre, she was going to bring her back instantly, whether Colleen liked it or not.

76

eight
D

Kingsley and Lyndon doffed their hats to the ladies on the porch. "Ladies," they both said politely.

The women all nodded back.

"How's your mother doin', Kingsley?" Mrs. Chiles asked.

Kingsley's mother had an influenza that she couldn't seem to shake. The doctor had been very worried about her.

"Better, thank you, ma'am," Kingsley replied.

"Imagine, both of you comin' to see me," Colleen said with a coquettish smile.

The boys' faces were grim, and Colleen instantly felt contrite. Here she was flirting while they were about to march into battle. Her mother told her that she was too much of a flirt, but she always denied it. She figured her mother was just jealous because her own flirting days were behind her.

But maybe Momma is right, Colleen thought guiltily.

She looked from Kingsley to Lyndon, and sighed. She cared about both of them, but they certainly didn't care for each other. She and Kingsley had been good friends for years, ever since his family had

77

moved to Franklin from Chattanooga because of his father's business interests. Kingsley was honest and steadfast, the kind of friend you could always count on. Elenora was forever telling Colleen how handsome Kingsley was. Colleen knew it was true, but she'd thought of him as her friend for so long that it was hard to consider him as a beau.

Lyndon was completely different. She'd met him only a couple of months earlier, when he'd been visiting with his aunt and uncle while on leave. They'd met at church one Sunday morning. Her mind had wandered during the sermon, and she'd been idly looking around the sanctuary when her eyes locked with the eyes of a young man in the pew across from her. He was so handsome he took her breath away. She was certain she had never seen him before.

When the service ended, he'd made a point of getting his cousin to introduce them—it would never have done for him to just introduce himself. He'd called on her later that very day, and it had been the most exciting day of her life to date. Lyndon had read all the same books she had read. He loved poetry and could even recite it to her. And he played the piano so beautifully it brought tears to her eyes.

Kingsley's idea of literature was the penny serial drawings. It wasn't that he wasn't smart, it was just that his mind had a more practical bent. He planned to go into his father's business after the war. As for Lyndon, he didn't know what he would do, exactly. But he knew he wanted to travel, to see the world, to have great adventures.

And now, both of them were battle-hardened veterans of the War Between the States, ready to lay their lives on the line for their young country.

They had more in common than they knew. Both

of them had secretly confessed to Colleen that they believed Jefferson Davis should have emancipated the slaves at the same time Abraham Lincoln did. It would have been the smart thing to do. For both of them, the war wasn't about slavery but about their homes and their families, about states' rights and the Southern way of life.

"Could we speak with you down at the other end of the porch?" Kingsley asked Colleen.

She nodded, and went to the garden side of the porch, where it wrapped around the house, so they could have some privacy.

"I am happy to see both of you, you know," Colleen told them.

The two young men nodded uncomfortably. Both carried rifles with bayonets fixed to them. They wore identical, somewhat tattered uniforms of the Army of Tennessee. They both looked weary and in need of a shave. But Colleen thought them both indescribably handsome and dear to her.

In the distance, they heard more foreboding booms of cannon fire.

"A big fight's brewin', Colleen," Kingsley said, cocking his head toward the sound. "You can tell by the distant thunder."

"They're testing our picket line," Lyndon added.

Kingsley nodded. "The boys will hold. I know it."

"God will be with them," Colleen said fervently, "and with both of you."

The two young soldiers looked at one another, and their expressions turned sheepish.

"Well, that's just it, Colleen," Kingsley said. He pushed his dark hair out of his eyes and resettled his gray cap on his head. "We know that the good Lord is with us. But Lyndon and me, we wanted to know about you.''

Colleen shook her head. "About me? I don't understand."

"This fight that's commencin', it's going to be a big 'un, Colleen," Kingsley said. "Some won't make it."

"But you will," Colleen insisted. "You have to!"

"And me?" Lyndon asked.

"Both of you."

More cannon fire resounded.

Kingsley swiped one hand nervously through his hair again. "It's only hours away, Colleen. That's why I . . . we . . . had to come see you."

"Soldiers will die," Lyndon said sadly. "Our side, their side. That's what soldiers do."

Colleen hated the scary feelings that were washing over her. "You can't think like that, either of you. God and the Confederacy will protect you!"

"All soldiers believe that God is on their side, Colleen," Lyndon said, his eyes searching hers. "I often wonder. Do you think if you die in battle, it means that God doesn't favor you? But then how do you explain all the good and worthy young men who have died in battle?"

A particularly loud report echoed off the low hills surrounding Franklin.

"There's no time for all that," Kingsley snapped.

"I know philosophy isn't your bent," Lyndon replied. "You'd sooner murder in the name of righteousness than think about what it all means."

"Your insults are as meanin'less as you are," Kingsley replied. He turned to Colleen. "It isn't news to you that we don't care for each other. So you must be wonderin' what brought us here . . . together."

Colleen nodded.

"Well, the thing is . . ." Kingsley turned to look at Lyndon again. Then both young men turned to Colleen and blurted out the same words.

"I want to marry you."

Colleen's jaw fell open.

Lyndon reached for her hand. "I hadn't meant to ask you like this. Certainly not with him here. On this porch. While these beautiful hands were rolling bandages."

She looked down at the hand he was holding. It used to be beautiful. But now it was chapped from the cold, the nails ragged and broken from hard work.

"Your poetry is an insult," Kingsley scoffed. "Poetry won't keep Colleen warm or make her safe."

"Without poetry, there is no soul," Lyndon replied. "But you don't care about Colleen's soul, do you?"

"Is your poetry goin' to keep her warm?" Kingsley challenged. "How do you plan to support her? With sonnets?"

They glared at each other with hard eyes.

"Stop it, both of you. This is—this is crazy," Colleen managed.

Kingsley turned to her. "Don't you see? If you would only choose now, before we face the Yanks—"

"The one you choose will know he's not just fighting them," Lyndon went on, "he's fighting for your love."

Kingsley gave him a cold look. "And the one you don't choose won't go on with false hope anymore."

Colleen shook her head from side to side sadly. "It shouldn't be like this. When the man you love proposes to you, it should be beautiful, on bended knee."

Kingsley took her hand again. He cleared his throat. Flowery words, talking about emotions, didn't come easily to him. "Colleen, I've loved you ever since we went on that midsummer eve's picnic together, remember? We were twelve. Some boy put a frog in your picnic basket to scare you. But instead of gettin' scared, you ran after him and put the frog down his shirt."

Colleen smiled. "My mother sent me to my room without supper for that. She said it wasn't ladylike."

"You were always so strong," Kingsley went on. "And honest. And brave. And . . . and beautiful, too. If you'll do me the honor of being my wife, I'll always take care of you and our children. We'll have a beautiful home—near your parents, if you like. And . . . I'll be the happiest man on the face of the Earth."

His face was so earnest, so handsome and brave and honest. When he'd kissed her good-bye before going off to join the Army of Tennessee, she'd felt cherished and safe in his arms. The kiss had been exciting, but it hadn't swept her away like what she'd read about in books. And yet he was so dear to her.

"Oh, Kingsley—" Colleen began. "That was the sweetest—"

"Colleen," Lyndon said. His voice was a soft caress, almost as thrilling as his kisses. For she had kissed him, twice. And for the first time she'd understood that silly word *swoon*. She'd felt like swooning in Lyndon's arms.

Kingsley turned away, as now Lyndon took Colleen's hand. "I can't promise you the things Kingsley promises you. The truth is that I'm not ready for a home or for children. But I am ready to love you. Passionately. With all my heart."

He gazed into her eyes, and her knees felt weak.

"I know you, Colleen," Lyndon went on, "in a way that no one else knows you. We're alike, you and I. After this war is over, your heart will long for adventure, not for boring hearth and home. You're not the kind of girl who should be chained to one place before she's ever seen the world. See the world with me, Colleen—the great concert halls, the great museums. Come with me. Be my bride."

There was another burst of gunpowder thunder as the Yankee cannon drew closer.

Kingsley swung around. "That was nonsense if ever I've heard it. Colleen is much too levelheaded a girl to fall for that stuff."

"I suppose you think she'd prefer marrying you and turning into a copy of every other young matron in Middle, Tennessee? That would be utterly sad!"

"I've known fellows like you before, Lyndon," Kingsley said. "The ladies like you, I understand that. They think you're excitin', what with your poetry and all. But would you be there if the money ran low, or the days got dull, or the baby was sick, night after night? Would you?"

Lyndon frowned. "I'm far from ready for all that."

"Yessir, you are," Kingsley agreed. "You're a fine sort to spend some time with. But you aren't the marrying kind."

"If by that you mean that I don't believe two people should stay together if their love dies, then you're right," Lyndon agreed. "But love doesn't have to die. Besides, Colleen doesn't want what you have to offer."

"How do you know what she wants?" Kingsley asked.

"I know her," Lyndon said simply.

"I know her a durn sight better than you ever

will!'' Kingsley exclaimed, jutting out his chin.

"Can't you both see how impossible this is?'' Colleen asked them. "Please don't ask me to do this.''

There was another blast of cannon fire, even closer. The ground shook.

"Sixty-four-pound Union shells; I can tell from the report,'' Kingsley said, his voice tense. "Our unit is fixin' to form up yonder.''

"There's not much time,'' Lyndon said.

"Choose, Colleen,'' Kingsley urged her. "Before the Yanks come.''

"Choose,'' they both said at once.

"How can I choose?'' Colleen cried. "Both of you are dear to me. I can't decide like this. It isn't fair!''

"Do you love both of us, then?'' Lyndon asked, his voice gentle. "Can you honestly say that?''

Yes, Colleen thought. *Not in the same way, but yes.*

"I want both of you to understand something,'' she said earnestly. "I'm not ready to get married.''

"It doesn't have to be the dull picture Kingsley painted, I'm sure of it,'' Lyndon said.

"When you truly love someone, I'm sure it isn't dull at all,'' Colleen said. "But you have to be ready to . . . to make a commitment before God, forever. Perhaps both of you are ready. But I'm not.''

"See, that's what I mean about how honest you are,'' Kingsley finally said. "How's about we rethink this, then? You can just pick your sweetheart.''

Lyndon nodded. "I agree, if that's what you want.''

"The marryin' part can come later, when you're ready,'' Kingsley said.

"I can't,'' Colleen said. "When the war's over—''

"Colleen, I'm askin' just this one thing from you,''

Kingsley pleaded. "Please, don't make me go into battle without knowin' where I stand."

"It may be the last thing either of us ever gets to ask you," Lyndon added.

Colleen turned away from both of them, tears in her eyes. How could she choose? Kingsley was more dear to her than anyone in the world outside of her own family. She would trust him with her life. But Lyndon was so exciting! How could she ever give up that kind of excitement? To think of sharing his kisses, and one day much more, night after night—it made her blush just thinking about it.

She couldn't choose. She couldn't. "I . . . I need more time," she faltered.

"There is no more time," Lyndon insisted.

"And it isn't fair this way, Colleen," Kingsley added.

He was right. She knew it. But she still couldn't do it. It was her eighteenth birthday, and she loved them both. She would not break her own heart, or either of theirs, by choosing.

Off in the distance, the drum and bugle corps of the Army of Tennessee began to play. All over the field in front of Carter House, Rebel troops jumped to their feet, extinguished their fires, and hurried off to join their units. Older men shouted, younger men gave wild rebel yells. A horse-drawn munitions wagon pulled up next to their side of the porch. One of the horses neighed.

"It's time," Kingsley said, his voice tense.

Lyndon nodded. "Please, Colleen, choose. We have to go."

The bugles and drums were deafening now.

Colleen looked into Kingsley's eyes, so dear to her.

She looked into Lyndon's, which promised such passion.

"I'm sorry," she told them both. Tears were streaming down her cheeks. "I'm sorry, but I can't do it."

All three of them were so intent they didn't see the spark from one of the campfires; it flew in the air on the breeze and touched against the munitions wagon.

They didn't see the wagon ignite.

And by then, it was too late.

The blast when the gunpowder exploded was earth-shattering, sending twisted metal, deadly shards of flying death, in all directions.

Lyndon died instantly. Kingsley died with Colleen's name on his lips. As for Colleen, she bled to death slowly, full of longing for the future she would never have.

nine

𝒟

"*Are you okay?*" *Betsy asked.*

Colleen nodded, and fisted away a tear that rolled down her cheek. She was sitting on her bed, cross-legged. "That was intense. It's not every day that you get to relive bleeding to death during the Civil War."

"I should have brought you back sooner," Betsy said remorsefully. "I couldn't decide if I should or not."

"No, you did the right thing," Colleen assured her. "I had to go through it. I had to know."

"Wait until you hear the audio," Betsy told her. "It must be incredible. You actually sang a song, Colleen. And get this: you sounded great."

"I did?"

"You did. Some song I never heard before. You were walking among all these soldiers, you said, and you started singing."

"No way," Colleen retorted, but Betsy went to the cassette player and rewound the tape from the session until she found the spot she was looking for.

Alberta, let your hair hang low.
Alberta, let your hair hang low.

*I'll give you more gold than your
pockets will hold.
If you'll only let your hair hang low.*

"Oh, my god," Colleen breathed. "That's me?"

Betsy nodded. "That's you. What song is that?"

"I have no idea."

"So how did you know it?" Betsy asked.

Colleen shrugged.

"Well, no offense, but Colleen Berendt has a lot better voice than Colleen Belmont. As you just heard."

Colleen shook her head. "But how is that possible? I mean, I have a terrible singing voice."

"I don't know how it's possible," Betsy said slowly. "But then, I don't know how the kids Moody talks about in his book could speak languages they'd never heard before, either."

Colleen shivered. "I have a feeling this is what Kevin would call the woo-woo stuff."

"Tell me about it," Betsy agreed.

Colleen got up and began to pace slowly across her room. "In the first regression, I went back to a lifetime in London during World War II, it was my eighteenth birthday, and I died. In the second one, I went back to a lifetime during the Civil War, it was my eighteenth birthday, and I died."

She turned to look at Betsy. They both knew her eighteenth birthday was coming up on January 1.

"It doesn't mean anything, necessarily," Betsy said.

"But what if it does?" Colleen asked, her eyes wide "What if—oh, God, Bets. What if it means I'm going to die on my birthday?"

Neither of them could speak for a few moments.

What Colleen had said was just too chilling.

"Remain calm," Betsy said. She took a deep breath. "Okay. Maybe it doesn't mean what you think it means. "Maybe it's—I don't know—it's just your mind's way of trying to work out bad karma or something."

"Nice try, Wu," Colleen said bitterly. She sat heavily on her bed. Her heart was pounding. "I could be about to die a horrible death in a week and a half."

Betsy went to sit with her. "We're not going to panic. Maybe Kevin is right and your imagination just made up all that stuff."

"Right," Colleen said. "And maybe I'll have Tolliver Heath's love child. But somehow, I doubt it."

Betsy got up and went to Colleen's bookshelf. She pulled down a thick textbook.

"What are you doing?"

"This is your textbook from American History I," Betsy told her as she flipped through the pages. "I wanted to see if there's anything in it about the battle of whatever town it was you were in."

"Franklin," Colleen told her. "Franklin, Tennessee. Wherever that is." She went over to the other bookshelf and pulled out an atlas.

"I can't find anything," Betsy said. "See? Proof that your fertile little mind just—"

"Here it is," Colleen said, pointing to a page in the atlas. "Franklin, Tennessee. A little south of Nashville."

"Okay, so there's some town named Franklin in Tennessee," Betsy said. She plopped herself back down on Colleen's bed. "That doesn't mean there was a battle there, or a whole bunch of Confederate soldiers hanging around campfires on some lawn in front of . . . Something House, whatever you said."

"Carter House," Colleen said. Her voice was heavy and flat.

"Yeah, that was it. Did you just remember?" Betsy asked.

Colleen went over to her and pointed to a side of the map of Tennessee in her atlas. There was a list of historic sites and other points of interest.

" 'Franklin, Tennessee: Carter House,' " Colleen read, her voice shaky. " 'Civil War battleground and museum. Open to the public.' "

Betsy nervously turned one of the studs in her left ear. "Okay, so it exists. You read about it somewhere, and the information stayed in your subconscious."

Colleen put the atlas back. "You don't believe that."

"Sure I do!" Betsy insisted. "Oh, I know. Your family drove to Florida on vacation last year. I bet you went through that town."

Colleen sagged against the wall. "The interstate went through Nashville. Not Franklin."

The room was eerily silent.

"We're just going to deal with this," Betsy finally said. "We're not going to freak. We're going to review everything Roni ever told either of us about regressions. And we'll read every single book we can get our hands on. That's a good plan, don't you think?"

"Would you think it was a good plan if those had been your regressions and your eighteenth birthday was in ten days?" Colleen asked.

"No," Betsy admitted. She had a pensive look on her face as she raked her fingers through her hair so that it went every which way. "There's got to be some clue in the regressions, something to go on."

"Besides my impending horrible death?" Colleen

asked. She shivered. Suddenly, she felt so cold.

Betsy bit her lower lip thoughtfully. "The great Wu mind is formulating something. Once Roni told me that sometimes people from this life can show up in the past. You know, as other people. Like you have to relive your karma with them, to work something out spiritually."

"Yeah, I think I read that in Moody's book, too. So?"

"So I'm thinking out loud," Betsy admitted. She got up to pace the room as Colleen had done before. "There were guys in both your regressions, right?"

"Right."

"Two guys in both regressions," Betsy went on, counting on her fingers. "During the Civil War it was Kingsley and Lyndon."

"And in England it was . . . let's see . . . Lawrence and . . . some old boyfriend who went away to war." Colleen shook her head. She couldn't remember his name.

"Karl," Betsy reminded her. "I remember because it's the same name as my crazy cousin in Saint Louis. You know, the one who raises homing pigeons that never come home."

"Can we stick to the subject here?" Colleen asked.

"Right. Okay. It's interesting how you were torn between two guys in both of those lifetimes," Betsy said. "That could be significant."

"Like how?" Colleen asked.

"Like I don't know how, but let's think about it," Betsy said. "You had to choose who you loved, right? That sounds like a big karma-type thing to me. Go over the details."

Colleen tapped one finger against her lips thoughtfully. "In England I had dumped Karl for Lawrence.

But I realized right before I died that I didn't really love Lawrence at all.''

Betsy nodded. "And during the Civil War, you loved both Kingsley and Lyndon, and you refused to choose.''

Colleen threw her hands up. "So there's no connection!''

"Maybe there is," Betsy insisted thoughtfully. "You had this passion thing going on with Lawrence, but you loved Karl. And you chose Lawrence, even though you realized at the end that it wasn't true love.''

"And I was passionate about Lyndon, but truly loved Kingsley, and I didn't choose. . . .''

"Well—I'm not saying this is true, Colleen, it's just an idea, so don't bite my head off. But what if the fact that you died had something to do with what was in your heart?''

Colleen thought for a moment, and what flew into her mind literally took her breath away. Then she gasped and sat heavily on her bed.

"In both dreams, I didn't choose my true love," she said. "In one I chose wrong, and in the other I refused to choose at all, and both times I died a horrible death.'' Colleen looked at Betsy. "Are you thinking what I'm thinking?''

"I have a feeling I am," Betsy said.

"Maybe if I had chosen my true love, I would have lived," Colleen said, her voice hushed.

Betsy nodded, mute.

"If I had chosen my true love," Colleen went on, her voice very small, "I wouldn't have been in that exact place at that exact time . . . and I would have lived.''

"Well," Betsy began slowly, "if it's true, then

everything is okay. Because this time around, you know the deal. And all you have to do is choose your true love on your birthday.''

Colleen's face drained of color.

"What?" Betsy asked. "You know who you love. Don't you?"

Colleen didn't move a muscle.

"Colleen? Say something, you're scaring me."

"My birthday is in ten days," Colleen began slowly.

"And you'll spend it with Kevin, the guy you love, right?" Betsy asked.

"I do love Kevin," Colleen agreed, her voice sounded strange and far away.

"Whew." Betsy threw herself back on the bed. "You gave me a minor heart attack there for a minute."

"But, Betsy," Colleen went on in that same strange voice, "when I look into my heart, there's someone else there, too."

Betsy sat up again. "No."

"Yes," Colleen insisted. "Luke." Now she finally looked at her friend, and her eyes were brimful with tears again. "And, Betsy, I don't know which of them I love more."

ten

"$\mathcal{M}$erry Christmas, sweetie," Mr. Belmont said to Colleen as she padded downstairs rubbing sleep from her eyes. It was still dark outside.

"Merry Christmas, darling!" her mother echoed. Mrs. Belmont was placing a silver-wrapped gift under their huge Christmas tree. "I'm glad to see that even though you're almost eighteen, you still keep the family's early-morning Christmas tradition." She gave Colleen a warm hug.

"My little girl will never be too old for a family Christmas," her father said, and he kissed her.

Because this may be the last Christmas that your little girl is still alive, Colleen thought. Then she banished the thought to the farthest corner of her mind. It was just too crazy. It couldn't possibly be true.

Kat padded out of the kitchen holding a mug of hot cider. "Why do you wear that uggo robe?" she asked Colleen, wrinkling her nose. "You look like a homeless person."

Colleen looked down at her old, ratty, red-flannel robe, her favorite. "It's comfortable."

Her mom peered at it. "What's that on the lapel,

Colleen? Why, it's that cameo pin you found at the thrift shop, isn't it?''

Colleen looked down. She couldn't remember pinning the cameo to her robe. Why would she do that?

"Dorky," Kat said, sipping her cider.

"It's Christmas, Kat," her mother said. "Don't call your sister dorky."

Colleen decided she must have pinned the cameo on her robe so that she wouldn't lose it, since she was forever misplacing her jewelry. That had to be it. This was another thought she decided to banish to a little back corner of her mind.

"To show how sorry you are for calling your sister names, why don't you get her a cup of coffee, Kat?" her father asked.

"She's got legs," Kat replied.

"It's Christmas, honey," her father said wryly. "Stretch a little."

Kat made an audible noise of disgust, but she went into the kitchen for the coffee.

Colleen plopped down on the couch as her father stoked the burning logs in the fireplace. She wrapped herself up in the afghan from the back of the couch. "How cold did it get last night? My room was freezing."

"Ten below," her mother said. "It's not supposed to get above zero today."

"But Mom and I already ran four miles," Kat said, coming back into the living room with Colleen's coffee.

"Hard core," Colleen commented.

Kat punched an imaginary forehand volley in her direction. "No guts, no glory, know what I mean?"

"That's my champion," her mom said, smiling at Kat.

I could win the Pulitzer for journalism and she wouldn't smile at me like that, Colleen thought. She pulled the afghan around her and took a sip of her coffee.

For as long as she could remember, her family had celebrated Christmas the exact same way. On Christmas Eve, they went to a midnight mass at St. Ignatius Church. Then, on Christmas morning, they all woke up before dawn to open their presents. And then, for midday dinner, they went to either the Belmont family reunion in Wausau or the McInerney family—Colleen's mother was a McInerney—gathering in Chicago.

Colleen stared into the blaze in the fireplace, lost in thought. Ever since her last regression, her emotions had run from one extreme to the other. Writing down a narrative of her experience, which she had done on her computer soon after, had done nothing to calm her nerves.

Sometimes she really believed that she was going to die on her eighteenth birthday, no matter what. Sometimes she thought that she'd live, if she could only figure out who she really loved, Kevin or Luke. And sometimes she thought the whole thing was just totally ridiculous and she was freaking herself out for nothing.

Kevin had wanted to know what happened at her second regression, and she'd been deliberately vague at first. But then one night after they'd seen a really romantic movie together, she told him everything.

Well, almost everything. She certainly hadn't told him that she and Betsy thought she had to pick her true love on her eighteenth birthday or she might actually die.

Kevin's reaction to her regression had been pretty

much like his reaction to the first one. He thought it was all just a figment of her imagination, and he said he wished she would give it a rest.

As for Luke, she hadn't seen him at all during the last couple of days before Christmas vacation had started. She thought about asking around to find out whether he was even at school, but forced herself not to. She had pretty much convinced herself that what she'd told Betsy, about not knowing if she loved Kevin or Luke, had been just temporary insanity on her part.

Of course, I don't love Luke, she thought now, as she stared into the fire. *I don't even know the guy. I'm totally over my stupid little infatuation.*

"When do we open the presents?" Kat asked, eyeing all the gaily wrapped gifts under their tree.

"After breakfast, like always," her father said.

"Mom and I had muffins right after our run," Kat said. "High fiber, no sugar, low salt, all natural."

"So's cardboard," Colleen said, "and that's probably what they tasted like." She got up from the couch. "How about if I make waffles?"

"How sweet of you, Colleen!" her mom exclaimed. "Only a half of one for me, honey," she added hastily.

"I'll eat the other half," Kat said. "No butter, no syrup. I'm in training."

"Good girl," her mother approved. "Your willpower is amazing, Kat."

Mrs. Belmont beamed at Kat, and Colleen felt as if she'd been trumped by her little sister yet again. She went into the kitchen to make the waffles that basically only she and her father would eat.

* * *

"Now?" Kat asked as soon as Colleen put her last bite of waffle into her mouth. She had polished off her half of a waffle ten minutes before. "Can we open them now?"

"Now," Mr. Belmont said with a laugh.

Kat tore into the living room and began to rip the wrapping paper off a giant box with a red ribbon.

"We take turns, remember?" her father said, kneeling down by the tree.

"Wow-ee!" Kat yelped as she lifted the lid on the box. "Yamaha sent me six more free rackets!"

"Oh, Kat, they must think you're going to be a star," Mrs. Belmont said with excitement.

"Well, I am." Kat took out a racket and balanced it upright on her palm. "And they stenciled the letter *K* on the strings. This is so cool!"

Colleen picked up a present and handed it to her father. "This one's from me, Dad," she told him.

His eyes lit up as he opened the box; it was a book about the history of money that was currently on all the best-seller lists.

"Thanks, sweetie," he said, kissing her cheek. "I've really been wanting to read this."

That's one Christmas present that I won't be borrowing to read, Colleen thought. But it made her happy to see how happy it made him.

One by one, they took turns opening their gifts. Kat's big gift from her parents was a new CD player she'd wanted desperately—and a gift certificate to a music store so that she could pick out some CDs. Colleen got a beautiful antique pin. And best of all, she got her own set of keys to the family car, plus a card that said if she earned half the money for car insurance, her parents would pay for the other half and buy her a used car of her own.

"So, what did tall, dark, and dorky give you?" Kat asked Colleen as she took a few practice swings with one of her new rackets.

"A muzzle for you," Colleen replied.

Kat laughed. "I bet he didn't give you anything."

"We're exchanging gifts tonight. He's stopping over after we get back from dinner."

Kat picked up the only gift still left under the tree. "Well, this came in the mail a couple of days ago and I stuck it under the tree. It has your name on it." She handed the small silver gift-wrapped box to Colleen.

Colleen turned the box over. "I don't know who this is from."

"Betsy?" her mother guessed.

"We exchanged gifts yesterday," Colleen said. She'd given Betsy a sweater that she knew Betsy had been wanting forever. And Betsy had given her a tiny guardian angel on a silver chain that already hung around her neck.

"Hey, there's a little card tucked under the flap of the wrapping paper," Kat pointed out.

Colleen took out the card and opened it. She read it out loud: " 'From someone who cares.' "

"Kevin, I knew it," Kat said. "He's such a dork."

"It probably is a surprise from Kevin," her father agreed. "Open it."

Colleen tore it open. It was a compact disc by a singer she'd never heard of, Carol Ponder. *Pretty Bird*, the jewel box read. There was a picture of Carol Ponder's face on the cover, and two words popped into her head when she looked at the picture. *Classic. Grand.*

"Who's Carol Ponder?" Kat asked, looking over Colleen's shoulder.

"I don't know," Colleen admitted.

"I'll bet it's love songs from Mr. Ugly and Disgusting Kevin," Kat said. "Can I play it on my new CD player?"

"No," Colleen said. "I'm going up to my room to listen to it. And then I'm going to call Kevin to thank him. And if you listen at my door or pick up the phone to listen into my conversation, I'm going to cut every string on your new rackets."

"Colleen," her mother chided her.

"You have no respect for greatness," Kat told Colleen. "When I get interviewed for *Sports Illustrated*, I'm going to say that I'm an only child."

Colleen didn't bother with a comeback. She just bounded up the stairs to listen to the CD.

Odd, she thought, as she sat on her bed, turning the gift over in her hand, *there's no cellophane around it.* She chuckled. *Maybe Kevin listened to it first.*

She popped the case open. Under the CD was a small orange Post-it note with a few words scrawled on it.

Wear the cameo when you listen to this. L.

Colleen froze.

Luke.

Her heart went for a little roller-coaster ride through her stomach. Her lips felt tender, as though he had just kissed them for hours.

"Luke," she whispered. She looked down at the CD.

"It's just some music," she told herself aloud. "It's not like it's a personal gift or anything. So just listen to it, and then write him a friendly and not very personal thank-you note."

She put the CD in her player, powered up her receiver, and pressed the play button.

> Alberta, let your hair hang low.
> Alberta, let your hair hang low.
> I'll give you more gold than your
> pockets will hold.
> If you'll only let your hair hang low.

Carol Ponder's voice filled the room, her a cappella singing so powerful it took Colleen's breath away.

"How?" Colleen whispered. "How did you know about the song, Luke?"

But Luke wasn't there to answer her.

> Alberta, what's on your mind?
> Alberta, what's on your mind?
> Your eyes are like twin pools of fire
> in the night.
> Alberta, what's on your mind?

Colleen wrapped her arms around herself, her eyes closed. And then, as Carol Ponder's majestic voice continued to sing, Colleen began to sing with her.

> Alberta, let your hair hang low. . . .

She could see the Confederate soldiers in their raggedy uniforms all around her; she could feel their raw fear—and their bravery, too. And their pride. She could see herself walking among them, singing that very song because she couldn't think of anything else

to do for them before they marched off to fight . . .
and to die.

It was real. It wasn't just her imagination. She had
been there.

And somehow, Luke knew.

eleven

*"**I** am the world's worst skater,"* Colleen moaned as she, Kevin, Betsy, and Betsy's ex-boyfriend Brandon (who had called Betsy on Christmas Day and begged for another chance) walked from the parking lot toward the frozen pond at the center of oh-so-imaginatively named Lakeside Park. "Why do I do this?"

She was in an irritable mood because she hadn't been sleeping well. Also, she'd called Tolliver at home again that morning, just as she had three other times since winter vacation began, to try to reason with him about starting up her paranormal column in the school paper. As usual, he had shot her down.

"Because it's fun," Kevin told her, draping one arm around her shoulders.

"I have weak ankles, I hate the cold, and I'm afraid of falling," Colleen grumbled. "For me, ice skating is an exercise in humiliation. The movies, now, that's fun."

"Hey, you only fell twenty or thirty times when we went last winter," Betsy said.

"And you didn't fall through the ice once," Brandon teased.

"How comforting to have such supportive friends," Colleen said. "I was hoping that the pond wouldn't freeze this winter, and I could skip my annual humiliation on ice."

"This is Wisconsin, Belmont," Betsy said. "Dream on."

They sat down on a bench to put on their skates.

"Hey, I have an idea," Kevin said brightly as he looped the laces of his skates. "I'll get you roller blades for your birthday and you can practice up over the summer."

"Swell," Colleen said, laughing.

"Yo, be nice to my best friend or she'll come to my New Year's Eve party with someone else," Betsy threatened.

Betsy was only teasing, but Colleen saw Kevin's face get tense. Ever since that stupid thing with Luke, he hadn't felt as sure about her, she could tell. She nuzzled against him. "Hey, you're definitely my guy under the mistletoe when the clock strikes midnight," she assured him.

"And then it turns from a New Year's Eve party into your birthday party," Betsy said. "Two unbelievably cool parties in one."

She and Colleen traded looks. They'd had endless discussions about Colleen's regressions and whether or not Colleen was actually going to be in danger on her birthday. Roni, who had come home for the week between Christmas and New Year's, had reassured Colleen that she'd never seen or read about, in all her experience, anyone who had died over and over at the exact same point in her past lives, so it had to be plain old coincidence.

Colleen was pretty much convinced. So was Betsy.

But "pretty much" still left room for doubt. Which

was what kept Colleen awake at night, tossing and turning, her fears magnified into night terrors. She'd see herself dying some gruesome death from which she could not escape. Only when the day began to dawn could she fall into an uneasy sleep.

"I'll be glad when it's January second," Betsy told Colleen. "All of this will be over."

Colleen nodded. "And I can finally get some sleep."

It was a frigid, sunny afternoon, two days after Christmas. There were dozens of colorfully dressed skaters of all ages gliding around the pond to the music from the sound system at the makeshift snack bar. Other people sat on the green benches that surrounded the pond, or stood near the snack bar talking and sipping hot chocolate.

"Ready to rock and roll?" Betsy asked Brandon as she stood up on her skates.

"Lead the way," Brandon replied.

Betsy took his hand, and they slid out onto the ice.

Colleen watched them as they skated hand in hand. Then Betsy skated backward, obviously carrying on an animated conversation with Brandon at the same time.

"Betsy is such a great athlete," Colleen said to Kevin wistfully.

"You could be, too, if you had any interest in it," Kevin told her.

Colleen shook her head no. "Kat and my mom are the athletes in my family. I'll stick to movie reviews."

Kevin got up and held out his hands to her. "Ready?"

"As ready as I'm gonna get." She took his hands, and they hit the ice. She wobbled immediately. Kevin helped keep her steady. "I hate this." She groaned.

"Don't think about it so much," he coached. "You tense up, and then you fall. It's like a self-fulfilling prophecy. Relax."

She tried. Her ankles kept threatening to turn, and she felt sure she was going to land on her butt at any moment. "I'm hardly a picture of grace," she told Kevin.

"You're doing fine," he assured her, holding tightly to her hand. "I won't let you fall."

"Looking good, Belmont," Betsy called as she whizzed by. "You're just about ready for the winter Olympics."

"Very funny," Colleen called back to her.

"Want to learn to skate backward?" Kevin asked.

"You're about as funny as Betsy."

"It's not hard, Col," Kevin insisted. "Here, just turn around and—"

"No, I can't—"

"Just relax—"

"I—eek!" Her legs went out from under her, and she landed hard on her butt. A toddler in a pale blue snowsuit skated smoothly around her.

"Perfect," Colleen muttered, red-faced.

"Ice one, Belmont zip!" Betsy commented.

"Go, Colleen!" Brandon applauded and whistled through his fingers.

"I don't feel like too big of an idiot," Colleen said as Kevin helped her up. She swiped the ice off the butt of her blue jeans.

"Yoo-hoo! Colleen! Kev-in!" a high female voice singsonged in their direction.

Colleen groaned. "Now my day is complete. It's the Curls." Colleen wobbled off the ice and hobbled over to the nearest bench. Kevin followed her.

Celeste Nan Durkey skated smoothly over to a stop,

blond curls flying. She was a vision in hot pink, from her knit cap to her skating skirt, right down to her skates themselves. She left the ice and came over to them. "Hi, you guys. Long time no see and all that."

"Hello, Celeste, and all that," Colleen said, her voice flat. "They have a fire sale at the Pepto-Bismol plant or something?"

"You know I believe in color coordination," Celeste replied. She took in Colleen's jeans, navy sweater, and ski parka. "Some girls will dress in any old thing, but others care about how they look. Gee, nasty fall you took out there, huh?"

"No biggie," Colleen assured her.

"I think it's brave that every winter you're willing to come out here and publicly humiliate yourself, Colleen, I really do," Celeste told her. "How did your little sister get to be a tennis star when you're such a klutz?"

"Chill, Celeste, huh?" Kevin suggested.

"Oh, I'm only teasing." the Curls' eyes lit on Betsy and Brandon out on the ice, playing a game of speed-skating tag. "Oh, gosh, they're back together? I thought he dumped her for some cheerleader from Brown Deer High."

"He realized the error of his ways," Colleen told her.

Celeste twisted one curl around her finger. "Brandon is hot. Betsy wears clothes from thrift stores and has a navel ring. What could he possibly see in her?"

"Brains, personality, looks, all the things you lack?" Colleen asked brightly.

"Can we just go skate?" Kevin asked.

"One life-threatening wipeout is plenty for me, thanks," Colleen said, unlacing her skates. "Besides,

Celeste was just leaving. Right Celeste? 'Bye, Celeste. Thanks for darkening our—''

"Hello, fellow Lakesiders," Tolliver Heath's unctuous voice said as he walked over to them from the direction of the snack bar. He was the only person in sight wearing a navy cashmere coat and dress trousers.

"Did you get my hot chocolate, Tollie?" Celeste asked.

"The line is endless, I'll get you one later on." He pushed his glasses up his nose and looked at Colleen. "And did we all have a delightful Christmas?"

"You asked me that on the phone this morning, Tolliver," Colleen reminded him.

Celeste narrowed her eyes. "What were you doing calling her?"

"Just begging me to run away with him, Celeste," Colleen said. "Be sure to print that in your column when school starts up again. It's just about as true as everything else you write."

Celeste folded her arms. "If you're referring to the tiny item I wrote about you and Luke, it was the truth. You were alone with him in the auditorium, so don't deny it."

"That doesn't mean we were doing anything other than talking," Colleen said, her temper flaring.

"You're so into him, Colleen," Celeste insisted. She cut her eyes over to Kevin. "You'd jump his bones if a certain someone wasn't in the picture. Everyone knows it."

Kevin scowled. "I'm going to get some coffee." He walked away on the toes of his skate blades.

"Kevin—" Colleen began, instantly sorry that she'd given Celeste an opening to bring up Luke.

Kevin gestured that she should leave him alone, and kept walking.

"Oops. Was it something I said?" Celeste asked, innocently.

Colleen smiled sarcastically. "Thanks, Celeste. I can always count on you for a 'We Are the World' moment."

"Ladies, this is not exactly the Christmas spirit," Tolliver lectured.

Colleen turned on him. "How can you run her stupid, lying, insulting piece-of-crap gossip column and not run my paranormal column?"

"My column is not stupid," Celeste said, tossing her curls.

"Right," Colleen agreed. "It's *sub*-stupid. Which pretty much sums up your mind and your personality."

"Jealousy doesn't suit you, Colleen," Celeste said. She kissed Tolliver's cheek. "I'm going to the potty. Back in a sec."

Colleen made a noise of disgust and pulled off her skates. "You two deserve each other, Tolliver."

Tolliver sat down next to her. "Did you think we were together? We're not."

"Did you think I cared, Tollie?" She looked over her shoulder at Kevin, who was in line at the snack bar, his hands buried in his pockets.

"We're not romantically involved is what I meant," Tolliver explained. "Celeste and I are merely friends and colleagues." He hesitated. "I heard through the grapevine that she was telling people I invited her to the spring dance. That is an untruth."

Colleen just looked at him.

"I wanted to be clear," Tolliver added.

Colleen turned to watch Kevin again. She couldn't

decide if she should go over to him or if that would just make it worse.

"I couldn't help noting that you and Mr. Armour are having some problems of late," Tolliver went on.

"Mr. Armour and I will work it out," Colleen murmured, her eyes on Kevin. He was talking with Shannon Kiefer now. She was on the girl's swim team. She was cute. She and Kevin certainly had a lot in common.

"Yes. Well, should you be facing the demise of your relationship," Tolliver went on, "I was thinking that perhaps you'd like to go to the spring dance with me."

That got Colleen's attention.

She turned to her editor. "Did you just ask me out, Tolliver?"

"Not exactly," Tolliver replied, pushing his glasses up again. "But Mr. Armour is hardly in your intellectual league, Colleen. It's only a matter of time before—"

"I love Kevin. And I'm going to the spring dance with him."

Tolliver nodded. He looked out at the skaters. "It's too bad about your column, Colleen. As editor in chief, I, of course, have veto power over everything that gets printed. And I have to do what's best for the newspaper. But perhaps I could be persuaded to change my mind. That is, if it was worth my while."

Colleen couldn't quite believe he meant what she thought he meant. "Could you be a little less obtuse?"

"Just that if you would like to change your mind about who is escorting you to the spring dance, I could perhaps change my mind about trying out your column."

"A date for a column, is that it?" Colleen was so angry, her hands shook. "If I told the principal what you just said to me, your butt would be toast, Tolliver."

"It would be your word against mine, so I doubt it," Tolliver said, but he looked nervous. "All I did was ask you to a dance. There are no strings attached to the offer, I assure you."

"Thanks, but no thanks, Tolliver."

She got up to walk away, but Tolliver quickly put his hand over hers and stopped her. "Colleen. Just one more thing. About Luke Ransom."

"What about him?"

"I strongly suggest you stay far away from him."

"And I strongly suggest you do not even breathe in my direction, Tolliver, except as has to do with the school paper," Colleen replied, her eyes flashing with fury.

She pointedly looked down at his hand, which was still on hers, and he moved it. "Just remember that I warned you," he said. "Luke Ransom is dangerous."

"Right. Just remember that I warned you, Tolliver." She leaned close to him, her eyes cold. "Stay out of my face."

"Mmmm, you feel so good, Colleen," Kevin said as he ran his hands over the smooth skin of her back, underneath her jacket and her sweater.

They were standing on her front porch. It was very late at night. Kevin hadn't stayed mad at her for long at the pond. And Colleen had made a mental note to not bring up Luke, or anything remotely connected to Luke, anytime Kevin was around.

After the ice skating, they'd gone to see two movies, shared a pizza, and spent a half hour parked in Kevin's car in the Belmonts' driveway, talking and kissing each other.

"I really have to go in," Colleen whispered. "My parents are going to have a fit."

"It's worth it," Kevin cajoled gently. "I'll take the blame. Let's go park by Lake Michigan."

She laughed. "Right. It's after midnight now. They'll lock me up in my room if I go back out."

He kissed her forehead, her cheek, her jawline, and then his mouth found hers again. She gave herself up to the incredible feeling of being in his arms and lost all track of time.

The porch light went on.

"Uh oh," Colleen said.

The door opened. Her father stood there in his pajamas and flannel robe.

"Hi, Daddy," Colleen said, feeling like an idiot.

"Hello, Mr. Belmont," Kevin added, hoping his lust for the man's daughter wasn't written all over his face.

"We were just . . . talking," Colleen explained.

"In Braille, no doubt," her father said wryly. "According to my watch, your curfew was twenty minutes ago."

"I'll be right in," Colleen assured him.

"Betsy called at nine-thirty," her father told her. "She made me promise to tell you to call her when you got in, no matter what time it was. Consider yourself told."

"Thanks." Colleen kissed her father's cheek.

He held up five fingers. "Five minutes for the big good-bye," he insisted, and closed the door.

"Your dad's great," Kevin said, putting his arms

112

around Colleen again. "My father would have screamed and cursed us both out."

"That's not exactly my father's style. Unless the stock market tanks, that is."

"Well, when we have a daughter one day, I hope I'm as cool with her as your dad is with you."

When we have a daughter one day? Colleen thought. *Isn't he rushing things just a little?*

"I may never get married," Colleen said blithely. "No kids, either."

"You don't mean it," Kevin said with certainty.

Colleen shrugged. "Who knows? What if I want to be a war correspondent and fly off to Kosovo or Iraq or wherever the undeclared war of the moment happens to be?"

"Colleen, you want to be a movie critic."

"Well, I could change my mind. I'm just saying that my future isn't all planned out, okay?"

"Okay." His voice was cold.

"Are you mad?"

He shook his head no. "But sometimes, Col . . . I don't know. It's like I know you love me as much as I love you, but something about that scares you. And you pull away."

She gently touched his cheek. "I do love you. I'm just not ready to think about my future like that."

"It's not because of that stupid regression stuff, is it?" Kevin asked her. "I mean, you don't believe that you're going to die, do you?"

"It doesn't have anything to do with that."

"Good. I'm glad you're done with that stuff, Colleen."

She didn't say anything.

He kissed her quickly. "I'm outta here. I'll pick you up at noon tomorrow, okay?" They'd made plans to drive inland so that Kevin could take outdoor shots of her for his photography portfolio.

"Cool. 'Night. Drive safe."

She closed the door behind her and ran upstairs to her room. As soon as her parents heard her door close, the light in their bedroom went off.

There was a big note propped up on her dresser: CALL BETSY AS SOON AS YOU GET IN, ANY HOUR. DAD.

Colleen punched Betsy's number into her phone and sat on her bed.

"I've only been waiting for three hours," Betsy said when she answered.

"How'd you know it was me calling?"

"This late, it was either you or a dirty phone call," Betsy replied, "and I didn't hear any heavy breathing."

"And the ever-strict Mr. and Mrs. Wu are—"

"At a community center in Milwaukee," Betsy replied. "The homeless sleep there when it gets cold, and they volunteered to stay overnight, make them breakfast in the morning, and all that. But I did not call to talk about my socially aware parents. The thing is, I figured out your regressions."

"What do you mean?"

"I mean I know how to make sure you live to see your nineteenth birthday."

"Wait a minute. I thought you thought the whole death thing was ridiculous," Colleen reminded her.

"So I lied. What was I supposed to say, 'Yeah, I'm still pretty freaked that you might actually croak at the stroke of midnight on New Year's'?"

"Yes, actually," Colleen replied, back on her feet now, and pacing with the phone. "Now that you're worried, I'm worried, too."

"Fear not," Betsy assured her. "The great Wu mind has figured it out. Stay with me, here. During the Second World War, you had to choose between Lawrence and Karl. You chose Lawrence, you croaked. During the Civil War, you had to choose between Lyndon and Kingsley. You didn't choose, you croaked."

"So the answer is, if I live in a lifetime without a war going on, I'm safe," Colleen surmised.

"It's right in front of your face, Colleen," Betsy told her. "Both times you had to choose between a guy whose name started with an *L* and a guy whose name started with a *K*."

Colleen sat on her bed.

K. Kevin.

L. Luke.

"You still there?" Betsy asked.

"I'm here."

"One time you picked wrong and one time you didn't pick at all," Betsy went on. "But what you *didn't* do either time was pick the guy whose name started with a *K*. Get it? The *K* name is your true love. If you're with him on your birthday, you live!"

Kevin.

A smile spread slowly across Colleen's face. "Bets," she said, "you're a genius."

"So true," Betsy agreed.

"And I think tonight, finally," Colleen said slowly, "I'm actually going to be able to get some sleep."

twelve

✑

"*I'm really glad you're here, Roni,*" Colleen said gratefully as Betsy's sister went to dim the lights in Betsy's room.

"You should be," Betsy told her friend. "Because there's no way I would have regressed you again without my sister here. No, ma'am; no way, no how."

"I'm glad I'm here, too, actually," Roni said. "To tell you the truth, your case fascinates me."

It was now just three days before New Year's Day—and Colleen's eighteenth birthday. Betsy had told Roni all about Colleen's regression experience to the Civil War, and about the theory the two of them had come up with about why Colleen had died in her two previous regressions. Roni was skeptical. But she'd still agreed to regress Colleen again.

Betsy bit nervously at a hangnail. "Are you sure you want to do this again, Colleen? I mean, really, really sure?"

"How else am I going to know if your theory is right or not?" Colleen asked. "I figure if I regress to a third past life, and my true love is some guy with a *K* name, and I pick him, I'm home free."

"But what if you don't?" Betsy asked. "What if—"

"Betsy, you know that I don't allow negativity in the regression room," Roni reminded her.

"I'm not being negative. I'm being cautious."

"As I told you both before, it's my professional opinion that dying on her eighteenth birthday in the two regressions Colleen did was nothing more than a macabre coincidence. She is not going to die on her eighteenth birthday in a third regression. And even if she did, it has nothing to do with real life."

"You could be wrong," Betsy said.

"If you can't find serenity, you have to leave," Roni warned her sister.

"I'm serene, I'm serene," Betsy muttered.

"You don't have to worry about me, Bets," Colleen assured her. "Just remember, you can't tell Kevin about this."

Betsy nodded.

"Ready, Colleen?" Roni asked. She pushed a button that would start her videotape recording of the session.

Colleen nodded. "Okay." She laid down on Betsy's bed and closed her eyes.

"Good," Roni said. "Now, start your deep breathing, Colleen. Just relax. Relax and release all your tension."

As she had the two times she had been regressed before, Colleen breathed deeply and evenly while Roni talked her through the hypnosis sequence. The feelings Colleen experienced were now familiar—her body got heavy, her mind drifted, and the same lovely warmth enveloped and caressed her, washing away any anxiety that she might have had.

"Your body is getting very heavy now," Roni said.

"You are sinking deeper and deeper into a state of complete calm. You have no worries, no tension, only peace."

As Roni kept talking, Colleen felt herself at that golden place at Lake Michigan where she had gone the summer before with Kevin. It was once again a perfect day; she and Kevin were lying hand in hand on a blanket, their faces warmed by the sun.

Then she felt herself float upward, farther and farther. It was the most natural thing in the world to leave her body.

"Four, three, two, one . . ." Roni counted. "And now, Colleen, you are ready to come back down to Earth. You have no fear, no tension, only peace. You are perfectly safe. You are going, back, further and further back, to before your birth in this lifetime. Let yourself go freely, joyfully. Slowly, you will float back down. But when you safely land, you will find yourself in a previous life, one that you have already lived. You will be able to tell me what you experience. And you will know, most of all, that you are safe."

Colleen wanted to nod, but her head was too heavy.

"Accept what you see, Colleen," Roni's voice told her, "and tell me what you see. You are completely safe. You are completely, completely safe. Feel yourself float down to Earth now, Colleen. Safely and serenely, no worries, you float down to Earth."

Down.

Down.

Down.

Down.

And once again, contact.

*　　*　　*

Colleen looked around.

She was in a city, that much was clear. She was surrounded by tall buildings, and the wind was blustery and cold. She huddled against the wall of a grand building, trying to get out of the wind. Across the street was a park. On the street, horse-drawn carriages. Men wearing top hats, well-dressed ladies on their arms, were walking past her. The women wore long, fitted coats with fur collars and cuffs. Some warmed their hands in small, fur tubes.

Muffs, Colleen thought. *They're called muffs. How do I know that?*

A young couple walked by, laughing together.

"Oh, Jonathan, stop!" The girl took one hand out of her muff and hit Jonathan playfully on the arm. "You are terribly rude, you know."

"I beg your pardon," the young man replied, laughing again.

They were speaking English, clearly American. But it sounded so old-fashioned and stilted.

"Colleen?" Roni asked. "Where are you?"

"I don't know," she replied, shivering against the building. She felt confused, lost.

A strong gust of wind blew a few pages of a thrown-away newspaper into her face. She grabbed a page and read the headline:

PRESIDENT GROVER CLEVELAND TO VISIT CITY IN APRIL

She looked up at the name of the newspaper. It was *The New York Times.* "Sunday, March 11, 1888," it said.

"Colleen?" Roni called again. "Are you all right?"

"I'm in New York," Colleen said. And as she said it, her life came to her like a photo developing before her eyes.

"My name is Colleen," she whispered.

"Colleen what?" Roni asked.

Colleen shook her head sadly. "Just Colleen."

The winter had been so long and so cold. She had been sick through much of it, and even now her lungs ached with every breath she took.

"You must have a last name," Roni pressed. "Stay relaxed and it will come to you."

Colleen shrugged. "They all just called me Colleen at the orphanage. Or Red, on account of my hair."

"She's an orphan?" Betsy screeched anxiously.

"Shhh!" Roni hissed at her sister. "Do you live at the orphanage, Colleen?" she asked.

"No more." Colleen wrapped her moth-eaten shawl more tightly around her shoulders. There were holes in her lace-up shoes, and her dress was thin and thread-bare.

"Where do you live now?" Roni asked.

"Nowhere," Colleen replied. "I ran away from the orphanage four years ago. They were so mean. They hit us, you know? So now I don't live anywhere."

"She's homeless?" Betsy asked, biting at her hangnail again. "I don't have a good feeling about this, Roni."

Roni put one finger to her lips, warning Betsy to be quiet. "Colleen? As long as you can hear the sound of my voice, you're safe. My voice connects you to your life as Colleen Belmont. Will you remember that?"

Colleen laughed bitterly. She was reading a page of the newspaper she held. There was a big story about how the next day, March 12, was going to be

Spring Opening Day at all the grand and famous department stores on fashionable Fourteenth Street.

"Why did you laugh like that, Colleen?" Roni asked.

"There are spring sales at the fashionable stores tomorrow," Colleen said. "How very la-de-da. If it wasn't for the fact that I don't have a cent to my name, I'd pop in and pick up a few new dresses. And a diamond bracelet. After all, tomorrow is my eighteenth birthday."

"Oh, God," Betsy moaned, wrapping her arms around herself. "This is bad, Roni—"

"If you don't shut up, you are out of here," Roni hissed at her. "I mean it!"

Betsy sat in the chair in front of her desk and looked at her best friend.

"Everything is okay, Colleen," Roni assured her. "Just keep talking to me."

Colleen let the newspaper page fly off in the wind. She shivered, and tried to curl into herself. "I'm hungry," she said. "I'm so hungry. Lucky stole some apples from a vendor this morning. He gave me two—that's the last time I ate. He always makes sure I eat. Kip, too."

"Who are Lucky and Kip?" Roni asked.

"My friends."

"Are they with you now?" Roni asked.

"No," Colleen said. "Not now. I'm alone. New York City. With all the tall buildings around me." She coughed twice. "It's so cold here."

"You'll warm up if you move around," Roni said. "Explore the buildings."

"In a while, maybe," Colleen said. She coughed again. "I'm too tired now. I don't feel very well."

Betsy cut her eyes at her sister, sending her a silent signal to do something to help Colleen.

"Are you ill, Colleen?" Roni asked.

"I don't know," Colleen said vaguely. She looked up at the gray sky. "The newspaper says it's going to snow a little and then clear off. But it feels more like rain."

"What newspaper?" Roni asked, raising her eyebrows.

"*The New York Times*," Colleen replied, shivering.

"What day is it, Colleen?" Roni queried. "What year?"

"Sunday. March 11, 1888."

Betsy blew some air out from between her pursed lips. Roni gave her a reassuring look.

"Where, exactly?" Roni asked.

Colleen looked down. Right at her feet was an advertising card for the grand building against which she was now huddled. She picked it up in her nearly numb fingers.

" 'The Fifth Avenue Hotel,' " she read aloud, " 'Madison Square, New York, has a world-wide reputation for refined cuisine, for its convenient situation, for its scientific ventilation, for everything a traveler needs. Each corridor has an iron fire escape from top to bottom. Earling, Griswold and Company, Proprietors.' "

"That's where you are?" Roni asked.

"I read it from their advertisement," Colleen explained. "I was the best reader in my class in grammar school."

"Where was that?" Roni asked.

Colleen tried to recall. "I can't remember. Before the orphanage. A long time ago."

Roni could actually hear Colleen's teeth chattering.

"Can you go inside the hotel to warm up?" Roni asked.

"No," Colleen said. "They throw vagrants out, or call the law on you. If I had thirty dollars I could stay the night there. Wouldn't that be lovely? I'll bet there are feather beds. And pillows filled with goose down. It must be so warm and lovely . . ." Her voice began to drift off.

Betsy jumped up. "Colleen?" she called, panicked. "Are you okay?"

Roni stabbed her finger at Betsy's chair, a murderous look in her eyes. Betsy sat.

"Breathe deeply, Colleen," Roni said, her voice calm. "You can feel the cold but at the same time you know that you are removed from it. Do you understand me?"

"Removed?" Colleen asked. She coughed again. Her mind was feeling fuzzy. She tried to recall who she was talking to. No one was around.

"You need to feel assured that you're safe," Roni explained.

"I—" Colleen began, but something down the block caught her eye. "Here comes Lucky. He's got food. I have to go."

"Don't stop talking to me, Colleen," Roni said quickly. "Colleen? Colleen?"

As Betsy watched Colleen, her friend's breath grew heavier.

"Maybe you should bring her back," Betsy said.

"Sometimes when a person is regressing they want part of the experience to be private," Roni explained. "It isn't dangerous at all, as long as they can still hear the voice of their regresser. I'm in complete control. The fact that she didn't answer me isn't something to worry about."

"You're sure you can bring her back at any time?" Betsy asked nervously.

"Totally," Roni said. "Watch." She turned to Colleen. "Colleen?" she called.

"Yes?"

"Would you like to return now?"

Colleen thought a moment. *Return where? Oh, of course. Roni. Betsy.*

But they didn't seem real. More like some dream she'd had. And Lucky was here. He had food.

"Colleen?" Roni called again. "You know that I'm with you and you're safe, no matter what. Even if you don't want to share everything with me right now, you know that I'm here, right?"

"Yes," Colleen said, though she was losing her train of thought again, unsure as to exactly what she was agreeing to. "I have to go. I'm so hungry. Lucky brought me a sandwich! Which makes me the luckiest girl in the world."

thirteen

Ʒ

*S*he had met Lucky a year and a half before, when she had slept under the Brooklyn Bridge one night and he had brought her a freshly roasted potato in the morning. He'd been with a friend of his, a boy named Kip, that same morning, and the three of them had become friends.

Colleen had no idea as to their real names—she knew them only as Kip and Lucky, just as they knew her as Colleen. She figured they were about her age, though their worldly eyes made them look older. Life on the street did that to you. Lucky had thick blond hair and blue eyes, and Kip's hair was as dark as his deep brown eyes. But both of them hardly bathed, so they kept their hair hacked off short with a knife Lucky had filched.

It was harder for rats and bugs to get into your hair when it was short. Girls who lived on the street knew that, too, and most of them hacked off their hair as well. Colleen knew she should. But the only thing she had left that made her feel like she was a person was her long, red hair. It had been beautiful once. Now it was a mass of knots and snarls. She kept it braided down her back, tied with a scrap of green ribbon she'd found in a rubbish heap.

The two boys looked out for Colleen as if they were her brothers, especially Lucky. They were the closest thing to family she had had in a very long time. This past winter, Colleen had been so sick that without them she doubted that she would have survived.

"Take it," Lucky said, thrusting a sandwich of some bread and meat roughly wrapped in newspaper into her hands. "Father Gilroy was giving them out near Grand Central."

Colleen stuffed a huge bite into her mouth. She felt as if she could eat a dozen sandwiches and still not get full. She finished half of it so quickly that it almost seemed as if she had imagined eating it.

Lucky looked at her closely. "How are you doing?"

"All right." She coughed deeply, her teeth chattering. "My birthday's tomorrow. Let's have a party."

"When did you last eat?" he asked softly.

Colleen was too busy chewing to answer, and her mouth was too full to even say hello when Kip came bounding across the street, dodging between the horse-drawn carriages. He was wearing his usual black overalls.

She swallowed and started to cough loudly as he approached.

"That doesn't sound at all right," Kip said sharply. He took off his ratty black scarf and wrapped it around her neck.

Lucky gave her a sad smile. "Hey, Kip. I wish we had some soup for her. At least it would warm her up."

"Well, I wish we had a feather bed and a quilt and

a thousand dollars in gold, but we don't,'' Kip said irritably.

Colleen sighed. That's how they always were—Lucky was tender and Kip was prickly. It didn't surprise her, really. Lucky had told her that he'd been raised by a wonderful mother and father, but they'd both died in the typhoid epidemic a few years before. Kip, though, never, ever talked about his parents. All he cared about was money. Getting it and keeping it.

What if one of them found some money one day? she'd fantasize. *It might fall out of a passing carriage on the way to a bank. If either Lucky or Kip had money, would they realize that I'm beautiful? Would one of them want to marry me and—*

Stop it, she told herself. *You're a filthy skin-and-bones thing who lives on the street. No one is going to be your Prince Charming. You might as well dream of sleeping at the Fifth Avenue Hotel. It's about as likely.*

''You need to see a doctor,'' Lucky told Colleen.

''Are you kidding, Lucky? Stop dreaming,'' Kip snapped. ''Any doctor in this city would throw us out of his office faster than month-old fish.''

''Sometimes a doctor comes by Trinity Church downtown,'' Colleen said weakly. ''On Broadway.''

''Too far,'' Lucky told her. ''You could never walk it.'' He sat next to her, rubbing her hands between his. A few raindrops splattered down from the cold, gray sky. The wind picked up a notch, too.

Lucky stuck his hands under the armpits of his threadbare sweater. ''There's the public soup kitchen in Chelsea, Colleen,'' Lucky said. ''We could try there.''

''It doesn't open for another hour,'' Kip said. ''And you can bet there's already a line to Long Island.''

"I'll be okay," Colleen said. She wanted to reassure them, but she could hear how pathetic her voice sounded. Suddenly, rain began to pelt down. All around them, people were scurrying for shelter.

Kip swore under his breath. "Coppers coming this way from the park. Let's move it."

Colleen got up quickly and staggered. Her two friends caught her, one on each side, and half dragged, half carried her west on Twenty-third Street to a loading area on the south side of the hotel. The area was blocked on three sides from the wind, and an overhang prevented most of the rain from hitting them directly.

Colleen sagged against the wall. "Thanks," she whispered.

"She's in bad shape," Lucky said.

"I got eyes, don't I?" Kip asked.

The rain fell harder, the wind blowing it into their little protected area. The boys put Colleen where the rain would least reach her. She still shivered.

"I've got to get you some hot food," Lucky told her.

"Hot food ain't gonna fix her up," Kip said. "She needs a doctor." He wiped the rain from his face and thought a moment. "Look, I know this old alkie who lives by the Chelsea piers. If I can filch a bottle for him, he'll come take a look at Colleen."

"What's he going to do?" Lucky asked.

"Before this guy was a lush, he was a doctor," Kip said. He started backing away from them. "If I can't find him, I'll . . . I'll think of something." He took off into the pouring rain.

Lucky knelt down and pulled the scarf more snugly around Colleen's neck. "A doctor," he told her. "That'll be good, huh?"

She didn't answer. They both knew they couldn't depend on Kip. Sometimes Kip came through and sometimes he didn't. If Kip couldn't find the doctor, or if he couldn't persuade him to come take a look at Colleen, Kip was likely to spend a few hours trying to pick some rich guy's pocket. He might or might not get caught. If he didn't get caught, he might or might not spend the money he got on a bottle for himself.

And then he might or might not come back.

Neither Colleen nor Lucky blamed him. On the street, you did what you had to do to stay alive.

"What if we had a home, Lucky?" Colleen asked dreamily, leaning her head against the rough gray brick of the hotel. "We'd have a fireplace, wouldn't we? And we'd sit around the fire, warming our hands."

"And a piano," Lucky said, going along with her fantasy. He wiped the rain from her cheeks tenderly. "I'd play for you."

"Do you really know how to play the piano?" Colleen asked, her voice barely a hoarse whisper.

"I did," Lucky said. "A long time ago."

Colleen tried to reach out for him. She was too tired to lift her arm. She smiled, but began to cough.

"I've got to get you some hot food and some help," Lucky said, his face etched with worry for her.

"Kip—"

"Yeah, Kip," Lucky said. "I love him like a brother, Colleen, but we both know he might not make it back here."

Colleen nodded, and coughed again.

"Look, I know you can't make it to Trinity Church," Lucky said. "I'm going to run all the way there and talk to the minister's wife. She cares about you, Colleen. She'll give me some food for you. And help. Maybe a carriage can come for you and take you there. Just until you're better."

She nodded again, too weak and miserable to speak.

"No matter what happens, Colleen, don't move from this spot. I'm coming back for you."

Colleen lifted her head and looked at him, her eyes huge. "Promise?" she whispered.

"I promise," he said fiercely. He tenderly touched her cheek with one finger, then pressed his lips to her forehead before he sped off into the pelting rain.

She was alone. She pulled her shawl over her head and closed her eyes. She didn't have the energy to cry.

In an instant, she was asleep.

Colleen awoke, fourteen hours later, to the Blizzard of '88. As for Lucky and Kip, they were nowhere in sight.

As the temperature had dropped, the driving rain of the evening before had turned first to sleet and then to snow. An intensely powerful low pressure system had made its way up the coast, and hugely strong winds rushed in to equalize the air pressure. The result was quite literally the storm of the century.

Winds whipped through the city streets at nearly a hundred miles an hour, carriages were tossed about like toys in the air, and all over the city, people were doing their best to battle the intense snow and wind.

Colleen was colder than she'd ever been in her life.

"Help?" she cried weakly. "Somebody help me?"

But the wind blew the words right back into her

mouth. She heard Lucky's last words to her echo inside her head.

Wait here for me. It could take a while. But wait.

She was exhausted. She closed her eyes.

Seven hours later, she awoke again.

This time, the city was literally buried in snow. Drifts five feet high or more had blown up against the buildings on the opposite side of Twenty-third Street. Nothing moved. No horses, no pedestrians, nothing. Even the ubiquitous pigeons knew better than to try to fly in the wind that continued to roar.

Colleen was so very cold. Beyond shivering.

I might die, she thought. But she was too cold even for that thought to scare her.

She closed her eyes again. When she opened them, it was an hour later, and she had the strangest feeling.

She was warm. All her pain was gone. Though she could feel the wind-driven snow lash her face, it felt more like fairy dust than like ice crystals.

She touched her nose but couldn't feel it.

Sleepy. She felt so sleepy. It would be so easy to go back to sleep, and when she woke up, she'd be in a magic place, far from the oppressive poverty of her existence in New York, someplace where it was always warm, where there was always food, and where she could hear Lucky playing his piano all the t—

"Colleen! Colleen!"

Go away, Colleen thought. *Let me sleep.*

"Colleen! Dammit, Colleen. *Wake up!*"

She opened her eyes. Someone was standing over her. She could barely make out the shape.

"Hi," she mumbled, and closed her eyes again.

Then she felt herself swept up in a pair of masculine arms, and the arms were carrying her someplace, steadily, quickly. She curled against the body.

"Colleen, don't sleep, don't!"

She felt the person carrying her open something—a door, maybe? Then she was in a building.

Warmth. Real warmth. There was a piano playing someplace. She opened her eyes cautiously.

She was inside the luxurious Fifth Avenue Hotel. Lucky had carried her in. They were just inside the lobby, and the hotel dicks had formed a rough semi-circle around them.

"What are you doing, young man?" one of the hotel police asked Lucky.

"What does it look like I'm doing? You need to take care of my girlfriend!" Lucky yelled. "She's dying!"

I am? Colleen thought. *No I'm not. I'm just tired. So, so tired.* But she didn't protest.

"Now see here," the hotel cop said, "this is not a place for vagrants—"

Lucky carried Colleen with him as he went nose-to-nose with the hotel dick.

"You see here," Lucky said to him, his voice colder than the weather. "Have you no decency, man? This girl is about to die! She needs soup! A bed! And now!"

"But we can't allow—"

"Of course you can!" Lucky roared, and his loud voice stilled all the others in the busy lobby. A concerned-looking man in a business suit hurried over. He was the hotel manager on duty.

"What seems to be the problem?" the man asked.

The detective looked disdainfully at Lucky and Colleen. "Them," he said contemptuously. "They're the problem. They think we run a charity institution here."

The man in the suit turned to Lucky. "Who are you?"

"We're two people a little poorer than you," Lucky said quickly. "One of us is dying. Now, if you'd like it in the papers that one of us expired in your lobby while the piano tinkled in the background, do nothing. Otherwise, for God's sake, man, help her!"

The hotel manager scratched his head, worried.

"Mr. Warmington?" one of the policemen asked him. "You want we should show these two the door?" He edged closer to Lucky and Colleen.

The manager shook his head. "No," he declared. "Go to the kitchen and get this young woman some soup. Corbett, you check them into a room. Many people will die because of this storm. This hotel is not going to be responsible for another of those deaths. And call the hotel doctor immediately to see this woman. What's her name, young man?"

"Colleen," Lucky said. "And thank you, sir."

"Thank you for giving me the chance to save a life," Mr. Warmington replied, and then he turned to Colleen.

"Young lady," he said, "you're going to be just fine."

Even in her torpor, Colleen managed a small smile. She was going to sleep in the Fifth Avenue Hotel. It was her birthday. She was going to live.

Obviously, miracles really *could* happen.

fourteen

D

*C*olleen opened her eyes. She was back in Betsy's bedroom, on the bed, facing the ceiling. She blinked a few times to clear her head.

"Breathe deeply, Colleen," Roni instructed her. "Let yourself come back to the now. Gently."

Colleen nodded and took a few slow breaths.

"Good," Roni said. "That was an excellent regression."

"Oh, yeah, it was swell," Betsy said sarcastically. "She stopped talking to you, scared the hell out of me, and nearly froze to death in the Blizzard of '88!"

Colleen sat up. Betsy sat next to her. "You okay?"

"Yeah," Colleen managed, though she still felt dazed. "Well, at least I didn't die on my eighteenth birthday in that lifetime," she added.

Betsy's face paled.

"What?" Colleen asked.

"Nothing," Betsy said quickly.

"Bets, your face is the color of typing paper."

"I think Betsy is reacting to the collapse of your joint theory about your regressions," Roni explained.

"Say that again in English." Colleen rubbed her temples gingerly. She still felt somewhat out of it.

"In English, I thought that if you chose your true love on your eighteenth birthday, you'd live," Betsy said slowly.

"And I did, he was—"

"Hel-lo!" Betsy interrupted. "Wake up, Colleen. His name was Lucky. As in first letter *L*. As in totally blowing my theory that your true love's name begins with a *K* in every one of your lifetimes, and if you're with said *K* guy on your birthday, you'll live."

Kip. Lucky. Kevin. Luke.

Suddenly, Colleen's mind focused, and her face drained of its color like Betsy's had. The two girls locked eyes.

"I admit it's fascinating that you always seem to regress to your eighteenth birthday, Colleen," Roni said. "But the fact that you didn't die in this regression should reassure you rather than scare you."

"It would, if Kip had been my true love and he'd saved my life," Colleen said. "But it was Lucky. *L*."

"I'm telling you, you are assuming a connection where no connection exists," Roni insisted. "Clearly, Lucky was a nickname, right? His real name could have started with any letter at all, as could Kip's."

"That's true," Betsy said hopefully. "For all we know, Lucky's real name could have been Ken."

Colleen nodded thoughtfully. "Which would mean my true loves' names all start with the letter *K* and—"

"You two remind me of a story I once heard," Roni said. "This guy insists he's the best archer in the world. To prove it, he shows everyone a target on the side of his barn. Every single arrow in it is in a bull's-eye. That's proof, right? Wrong. Because he shot the arrows first and then drew the bull's-eyes around them."

135

"Meaning we're freaking over nothing," Betsy concluded.

Colleen drew her knees up to her chest and hugged them with her arms. "I deeply hope you're right, Roni."

"I am." Roni popped the video cassette out of the camera. "Do you mind if I make a copy of your regression, Colleen? I'd love to have it for my files. And just to be sure, I'm going to do a phone consult with Marjorie Rathsmussen. She's a psychiatrist who studied with Dr. Moody. *The* Dr. Moody."

"Feel free," Colleen replied. She felt a sudden chill. "But I'm just praying that your theory is right, Roni. Or else that tape is going to be my epitaph."

Colleen sat in front of her computer the next evening reading the account of the previous regression that she'd typed after it was over. What Roni had said made a lot of sense, although she was still trying to reach Dr. Rathsmussen for confirmation.

Obviously, Lucky was a nickname, and Kip was probably a nickname, too. Roni had also pointed out that Colleen might have had any number of previous lives, so three regressions was hardly statistically significant.

Colleen began typing into her computer: "It bothers me that when Kevin came over last night I didn't tell him that I'd done another one. I hate keeping secrets from him—"

Knock-knock-knock on her bedroom door.

"Go away, Kat," Colleen called, and continued typing.

"But it's important," Kat said. She opened the

door and strode into Colleen's room. Colleen quickly blacked out the screen.

"What?" Colleen asked impatiently.

"When I'm rich and famous, you're going to regret that you were so mean to me," Kat said, folding her arms.

"I'll risk it. Now, what do you want?"

Kat took a deep breath. "Wendy's mom is taking us to the mall tomorrow and I have to get something to wear to Wendy's family's New Year's Eve party and this guy I kinda sorta like will be there and I don't know what to wear."

Colleen smiled at her sister. It was the first time Kat had ever mentioned a boy without using the word *dork* in the same sentence.

"Clothes that make you feel good," Colleen advised.

Kat shrugged. "A warm-up suit? Sweats?"

"Not sweats," Colleen said. "Jeans, if you want. And you could buy a new sweater. You look great in red."

Kat's face lit up shyly. "I do?"

Colleen playfully pulled down the bill of Kat's blue baseball cap. "You're growing up on me."

"Gag me," Kat said with a scowl, but Colleen could tell she was pleased.

Impetuously, Colleen went to her dresser and opened the top drawer, where she'd put the bottle of perfume spray her aunt had once sent her. Sunset Magic, it was called. She'd always thought that it smelled like a summer evening.

"Here," she said, handing it to Kat. "Wear this, too."

Kat looked shocked. "You're giving it to me?"

"Sure."

Kat smiled. "Thanks. Really."

"You're welcome, really. Now go away and let me work."

"Uh, just one other thing," Kat said. "I sort of borrowed that CD Kevin gave you for Christmas and I sort of left it over at Wendy's by mistake, but she's definitely returning it when I see her tomorrow, just in case you're looking for it."

"The Carol Ponder CD?" Colleen asked. "Kevin didn't give that to me. "A guy—a friend—named Luke did."

When Kat heard the name Luke, she grimaced.

"Oops."

"Oops what?" Colleen asked.

"Oops a guy named Luke called. I forgot to tell you."

"When?"

"This afternoon. You weren't home." She reached into the back pocket of her warm-up outfit and fished out a small scrap of paper. "That's his phone number."

"What did he say?" Colleen asked.

"Duh, to call him," Kat replied. "Oh, wait. He might have said right away. I suppose you're so ticked off that you're going to take back the Sunset Magic, right?"

Colleen pointed at the door. "Wrong. Good-bye."

As soon as Kat and her perfume left, Colleen picked up her phone and sat on her bed to call Luke. She hesitated. She hadn't given him her phone number. She hadn't even talked to him since before school let out for winter vacation. And she hadn't thought about him, either.

Well, not much, anyway, she added in her mind.

She caught her pensive reflection in the mirror over

138

the dresser and made a face at herself. "You are act-ing like an idiot," she told herself. "You sent him a thank-you note for the CD he sent to you. He called to thank you for the note. So just pick up the phone and call him back."

Right. She quickly punched his number into her phone and drummed her fingers nervously on her nightstand as the phone rang. And rang. And rang.

Click. "Hey," came Luke's taped voice through the phone. "You know what to do and when to do it." *Beep.*

"Hi, it's Colleen," she said, trying to sound much more casual than she felt. "My sister just gave me the message that you called . . . to say you got my note, right? So listen, thanks again for the CD. It's really great. No need to return this call. I'll see you back at school—"

Beep. His tape cut her off.

"Even your phone messages need an editor," she muttered to herself as she hung up. Well, that was that.

"Hey, Colleen!" Kat yelled through her door.

"Now what?" Colleen groaned.

Kat opened the door. "Some guy is downstairs for you."

"Tall, dark, and dorky?" Colleen asked.

Kat shook her head no. "Tall, blond, and barfy."

"You warm enough?" Luke asked.

They'd driven to the park and were now standing by the frozen pond. He hadn't explained why he'd showed up at her house or how he even knew where she lived. He'd just apologized for showing up on her doorstep and then asked her if they could go somewhere where they could talk.

"I'm fine," Colleen assured him, sticking her mittened hands into the pockets of her ski jacket. The night was biting cold and clear. All the stars were out.

"Did you have a good Christmas?" he asked her.

She turned to him and tried not to notice how hot he looked in his worn leather jacket and faded jeans. "You came over to ask me that?"

"No." He stared up at the starry sky. " 'There are more things in heaven and Earth than are known in your philosophy, Horatio.' "

"Ah, you came over to quote Shakespeare to me," Colleen said. "Everything is *so* much clearer now."

He continued to gaze up at the stars. "Lucky was lucky, don't you think?"

Colleen gasped as if someone had punched her in the stomach and knocked the wind out of her. "What . . . what did you just say?"

"Karl never did get to give you another bunny."

"How do you know about that?" Colleen whispered.

"You wouldn't have been happy with Kingsley," Luke went on. "Not that he wasn't a good guy, because he was. But dull. You needed passion. Lyndon could give you that."

"Tell me how you know these things!" Colleen demanded.

Now he finally turned to her. "I'm Lyndon," he said.

Her mouth gaped open. "You're—"

"And Lucky."

She could barely get her mouth to work. "And Lawrence, the violinist in London during World War Two?"

"That egotistical idiot? No. You didn't really love him. And as much as you were Karl's true love, he wasn't yours. I was Lawrence's younger brother, two years younger than you. I loved you, too. I thought you looked just like the beautiful ivory face carved in my mother's cameo pin. We met when Lawrence was playing a live concert on the BBC, remember? And he invited me and our mother because he thought it would look good for the photographers?"

Colleen searched her mind. "I don't remember . . ."

Luke smiled sadly. "I do. If only you hadn't invited Lawrence in for tea on your eighteenth birthday, you would have lived. We would have been so happy together."

"What—what was your name?" Colleen stammered.

"Lee."

Lee. Lyndon. Lucky. Her true loves. Luke.

L names. Not *K* names.

Colleen felt as if she couldn't breathe.

"We've been together so many times," Luke went on, staring out at the icy pond. "Remember in Korea in 1451? You were so sure Kim Il Kuk was the guy for you because you two were both servants and I was royalty. Remember how I defied my father and we ran away together?"

Colleen shook her head no.

"You didn't regress to that one yet, huh? We were so happy. For a while. Until you died in childbirth. And then I died of a broken heart."

"How . . . how can this be?" Colleen asked.

"I did my first past life regression three years ago," Luke explained. "When I lived in Chicago, I had a friend who was into it, and I tried it for a laugh.

Some laugh. I guess you could say that finding out about my past lives kind of changed my life."

"How many have you done?" Colleen asked.

"Lots, maybe two dozen. I've been rich and poor and everything in between. I've died all different kinds of deaths. But one thing was always the same."

"What?" she asked.

He turned to her. His electric blue eyes glinted in the moonlight. "You."

Colleen couldn't speak.

"I felt it from the moment that I first saw you at that jail laughingly referred to as Lakeside High School," Luke went on. "But what could I say? 'Nice to meet you, and by the way, we've been lovers since the beginning of time'?"

"But I love Kevin," she protested.

"You *think* you do," Luke said. "But how do you know?"

"I just do," Colleen insisted.

"Like you knew with Lawrence?"

She felt so confused, her head was spinning. She had no idea what was true anymore.

Luke's hand was on shoulder. Gently, he turned her to him. His eyes searched hers. "You feel it," he whispered. "I know you do. Search your heart. You'll find me there."

She couldn't tear her eyes away from his. She felt as if all this was happening to someone else.

Slowly, he brought his lips to hers. When he kissed her, she gave herself up to the kiss. His mouth scorched hers, and soon nothing mattered but this lifetime, this moment, and being lost in Luke's arms.

fifteen

It was the next evening when Betsy's mom let Colleen into the Wus' home. Colleen hurried up to Betsy's room. Betsy and Roni were expecting her.

Colleen hadn't slept at all the night before. When she finally got home, she crawled into bed, curled up into a ball, and lay there all night, eyes wide open.

I kissed Luke. And I liked it.

But I'm in love with Kevin. No, with Luke. No, Kevin. And I just cheated on him.

But Luke has been my true love through so many lifetimes. He proved it. Then why do I feel so guilty about kissing him and betraying Kevin?

Her mind had gone 'round and 'round, but no answers came. Finally, barely after dawn, she'd called Betsy and awakened her. Then she blurted out the entire story of what had happened the night before. Betsy had gotten Roni up, put her on the phone, and made Colleen repeat the whole thing for her sister.

"I feel like I'm losing my mind," she'd finally told Roni. "I don't know what to think or what to believe. And I don't know if I'm going to die the day after tomorrow!"

Roni had tried to calm Colleen down, and assured

her that she was still trying to contact Dr. Rathsmussen. She said she'd stay on it and get back to Colleen.

Colleen waited all day. Kevin called and asked her if he could come over to show her the photos he'd taken of her—they were dynamite. She said she wasn't feeling well.

Luke called twice. She let the answering machine pick up. She didn't call him back. Because she didn't know what to say.

Finally, Roni called her and asked her to come over. She had news. Now, Colleen strode into Betsy's room and turned to Roni. "What did you find out?"

"Take off your jacket," Betsy suggested, peering anxiously at her friend. "You look terrible."

"Thanks, I feel terrible." Colleen unzipped her jacket and threw it onto the bed.

"You'll feel calmer if you sit down and take a few deep breaths," Roni said.

"*You* take a few deep breaths," Colleen snapped, pacing the room furiously. "I'm sorry, I'm sorry, I'm just . . . I don't know *what* I am anymore." She forced herself to sit on Betsy's bed. "Okay. This is as calm as I'm going to get. Talk to me."

"I talked to Dr. Rathsmussen. She told me she just finished a huge study in past life regression under very controlled circumstances," Roni said.

"And?" Colleen asked.

"There was only one case similar to yours," Roni continued. "A young man, age twenty, did a dozen regressions, and in every single lifetime he died when he was twenty-one. Not on his birthday, but on the same date, March fourteenth."

"Did he live to age twenty-two?" Colleen asked.

"No," Roni admitted.

"Oh, God." Colleen's hand flew to her mouth.

"But it's not what you think!" Betsy exclaimed.

"It turned out that this young man was adopted," Roni went on. "He was removed from his parents' home when he was four. He and his little brother were abused by a stepfather. His little brother had died on March fourteenth the year before."

"But the guy didn't remember that, see?" Betsy explained. "It all came out afterwards."

Roni nodded. "He told the regressers the fourteenth had no special significance for him. And he was telling the truth, because all of this was buried in his subconscious."

"But that doesn't explain why he died on March fourteenth," Colleen said.

"He was drunk when he died, Col," Betsy said. "He drove off a bridge."

Roni cocked her head at Colleen. "Essentially, he killed himself. He carried a deeply buried trauma over what had happened to him and a terrible guilt that he had lived after his brother died—"

"So in his regressions, Rathsmussen believes, he died at twenty-one because he didn't think he deserved to grow up," Betsy concluded.

"None of that applies to me," Colleen said wearily.

"I think it does," Roni said. "I think if you did twenty regressions, you'd be struggling between two loves in all those regressions. It's your mind's way of expressing your anxiety over loving Kevin and Luke at the same time."

"But why do I die, then?"

"You don't, always," Betsy reminded her.

"Dr. Rathsmussen thinks the death part is just you punishing yourself out of guilt, like the young man I told you about," Roni said. "I agree."

145

"So . . . I didn't really die on my eighteenth birthday in those other lifetimes?" Colleen asked.

"Nope," Roni said. "The subconscious is very powerful. But it's critical for you to resolve your love life before I regress you again. And then you'll see that your imagining of your own death will disappear."

Colleen pushed her hair off her face. "What if you guys are wrong?"

"They're experts, Col," Betsy assured her.

"Right," Roni agreed. "Especially Dr. Rathsmussen. She wouldn't say she was certain unless she was certain."

"So unless you're so disturbed that you plan to off yourself the day after tomorrow," Betsy said, "you are home free, Belmont."

It made sense.

Slowly, Colleen smiled. She felt as if the weight of the eternal cosmos had been lifted from her shoulders.

"I may be thoroughly neurotic, but birthday suicide is not in my plans," Colleen declared. She looked over at Roni. "How can I ever thank you?"

"No need," Roni replied. "Dr. Rathsmussen told me about a fellowship opening in her department at Stanford. So you might have done me a favor."

Betsy threw her arms around Colleen and hugged her. "I'm so relieved. Aren't you?"

"Yeah," Colleen agreed. "Now, if I can only figure out who I really love, everything will be fine."

It was the mildest New Year's Eve anyone in Wisconsin could remember. The weather added to the usual fever pitch of the last night of the year.

As Colleen walked down the street to Betsy's, she

could hear loud music coming from Betsy's backyard. Some kids she knew were running around in various states of semidress. Two guys bolted barefoot through the front yard in their underwear—on a dare, Colleen figured—and one girl actually wore a bathing suit and snow boots.

The party itself was down at the lake's edge, in Mr. Wu's converted boathouse. Betsy, a master party-giver, had lit kerosene torches to form a path from her parents' front yard all the way down to the boathouse. And the trees were festooned with balloons, ribbons, and tiny white lights.

"Colleen!" Betsy spied her friend and ran over just as Colleen reached the top of the steps. "Is this wild, or what?"

Colleen peered at the insanity inside the boathouse. People were partying in every square inch of space. A couple slow-danced on an old coffee table, even though hip-hop music blared through the sound system. Under the table, another couple was crouched together, giggling, trying to lift it with their legs.

"Did you invite everyone in Lakeside?" Colleen asked.

"Just about," Betsy said, laughing. "Hey, it's New Year's. I say party hearty. How are you feeling?"

"Better," Colleen said.

"You're not freaked out anymore?"

"Let's just say my anxiety level went from off the scale to manageable. What Roni said makes sense. So every time I start to freak, I just remind myself that she's the expert and I'm just a victim of my own guilt about Luke and Kevin. Speaking of Kevin, is he here yet?"

Kevin had told Colleen that he attended a big family dinner every New Year's Eve, so they'd made plans to meet at Betsy's party as soon as the dinner was over.

"Haven't seen him," Betsy said. "But I saw Luke out back by the barbecue. Does Kevin know he's gonna be here?"

Colleen sighed and shook her head no.

"Does Luke know you're here with Kevin?" Betsy asked.

"No, and I haven't told Kevin about what happened with Luke—or that I did another regression." She held up her hands. "I know, I suck, you don't need to tell me."

"Then I won't," Betsy said. "You look really cute for the big showdown, though."

Colleen had on a crocheted lace dress with a matching crocheted sweater. She'd left her hair long and loose, and scattered tiny rhinestone clips through it. Around her neck she wore the angel necklace Betsy had given her for Christmas.

"You, too. Love the dress." Betsy had on a long dress from the sixties she'd found that morning at her favorite thrift store. It was a Gucci-type print, and the middle was cut out, exposing her navel ring.

"So, have you decided what you're going to do? Who you love, who gets a broken heart?" Betsy asked as a group of guys ran by throwing slushy snowballs at each other.

Colleen sighed. "No. Every time I think I've decided, I feel like I've decided wrong. I'm hoping that when I see Kevin and Luke, I'll just know."

"Yuh. Dream on, Belmont. So listen, there's everything from tofu to burgers on the grill if you're hungry. A bunch of people are on the lake ice fishing—I just hope the ice didn't melt, it's so warm. And

Brandon is threatening to cut a big hole and go skinny-dipping.''

"Did I hear my name?" Brandon asked, coming over to Betsy. He put his arms around her waist. "Did I mention that you're coming skinny-dipping with me?"

"You're delusional," Betsy said.

Brandon laughed and kissed her. Colleen was glad to see Betsy and Brandon back together. *Two guys for one girl may be highly overrated,* she thought ruefully.

"Hey, Belmont, the love of your life is here," Brandon said when he tore his lips away from Betsy's. "He asked me if you were here yet."

"Where's Kevin?" Colleen asked.

"Not Kevin," Brandon said, a mischievous glint in his eye. "Tollie. You know you want him."

"Betsy, you invited *Tolliver Heath*?"

"You want your paranormal column in the *Lakesider,* don't you?" Betsy asked.

"As Kat would say, gag me," Colleen muttered.

Betsy grinned. "The Curls is here, too. But strictly for amusement purposes."

Just then, Colleen felt a tap on her shoulder. She turned around. Luke.

"Hi." He gave her a heart-melting smile.

"Hi," she replied softly.

"Dance?" he asked.

Colleen hesitated. Now was the time to tell him that she was meeting Kevin at the party, that she loved Kevin, that the other night had been a huge mistake.

But the words wouldn't come out of her mouth.

"Oh, go dance, Colleen," Brandon said. "He didn't ask to marry you."

"Not yet," Luke added, softly enough so that only

she could hear him. He put out his hand. Colleen took it.

"Hey, cool, you guys!" Betsy cried. "Look out on the lake. Dinner is coming up through the ice!"

Out on the lake, brightly illuminated by a portable klieg light, a group of kids was gathered around a couple of ice-fishing holes. Someone was hauling a big lake trout through one hole while everyone else cheered.

Luke smiled and led Colleen inside the boathouse, which was packed with dancing bodies. The music was fast and hot, and they joined the teeming throng. Colleen lost herself in the music. If only she could keep dancing and not have to make any decisions.

The music changed to a Celine Dion ballad. All around them, couples began to slow-dance. Luke held her eyes with his. Then he held out his arms.

She wanted to walk into them. But it would be one thing for Kevin to find her bopping to Social Distortion with Luke, and quite another for him to catch her slow-dancing.

Tell him. Tell him now.

"I . . . Luke, I have to tell you something," she said. "I kind of . . . I have a date with Kevin tonight."

"Where is he?" Luke asked.

"He's meeting me here."

Luke smiled. "Of course. Two guys who love you. But only one is your true love. Just like before."

"But this isn't my birthday," Colleen said nervously. "It's tomorrow."

Luke looked at his watch. "Two hours from now, you mean. Happy New Year, and it's Colleen's birthday." He smiled again. "I waited lifetimes, Colleen. Believe me, I can wait two hours." He waved, worked his way through the crowd of dancers, and disappeared.

Maybe I should consider entering a nunnery, Colleen thought. *Eternal celibacy has to be easier than this.*

"Colleen," Tolliver said, sliding over to her. "You are looking very lovely this evening."

Be nice. Colleen gritted her teeth.

"Thanks, Tollie. Trust you to be the only guy here to show up in a tux."

He pushed his glasses up his nose. "Thank you. It's custom-made."

"Of course," she agreed.

Tolliver cleared his throat self-consciously. "I'd like to apologize for what I said to you at the pond a few days ago. Business and pleasure should be kept entirely separate."

"Apology accepted," she said, looking around for Kevin.

"Would you do me the honor of this dance?"

Slow-dance with Tolliver? That went above and beyond the call of duty. "Can't, Tollie. Gotta find someone."

"Kevin?" Tolliver said sharply. "How about Luke?"

"How about none of your business?" Colleen snapped. "Excuse me." She turned away from him.

"I'm just a big joke, aren't I?" Tolliver called to her. "Let's all laugh at Tolliver."

Colleen turned back to him. "If you are, you do it to yourself. Look at the way you treat people."

"Bull." Tolliver's prominent Adam's apple bobbed up and down in his skinny neck. "I have brains, family, money, and power. If I looked like Kevin or Luke, you'd be all over me. You're just as super-ficial as everyone else."

"Get a life, Tollie," Colleen said, turning away from him again.

He grabbed her wrist again. "I have to warn you, Colleen. About Luke. He's—"

"You are truly pathetic." She pulled her arm out of his grasp and hurried away from him. Just when she reached the door of the boathouse, Kevin mate-rialized.

"Hey, gorgeous," he said, giving her a hug. "Sorry I'm late. My grandmother is a big talker."

"I'm so glad to see you." She hugged him back. He felt so good, so safe and reassuring.

The music segued smoothly into another ballad. Kevin held out his arms. She melted into them, and they drifted together into the middle of the room.

This is where I belong, she thought as they swayed together to the music. *This is perfect.*

Across the room, something caught her eye. Luke was slow-dancing with a senior girl she didn't know. The girl was drop-dead gorgeous.

Jealousy punched Colleen in the gut.

Luke. Oh, Luke . . .

"Something wrong?" Kevin asked her.

"No, nothing," she replied quickly. "Everything is perfect."

Kevin pulled her closer, and they kept dancing. Colleen rested her head against his shoulder. But her eyes were squarely on Luke.

Betsy blinked the lights in the boathouse on and off several times and got someone to turn off the sound system.

"It's eleven-forty-five!" she announced. "I've lit the bonfire in the backyard, and I cordially invite you to come out and celebrate the first night of summer!"

Everyone laughed, and people mostly started moving toward the door, except for a few couples who were madly making out at the far end of the boathouse.

"Let's go out there," Colleen said to Kevin. "I love a bonfire at midnight."

Kevin shook his head. "I'll be out in a minute," he said. "You go."

Colleen got a sick feeling in her stomach. "Is there something wrong?" she asked.

Kevin smiled weakly. "Bathroom," he said glibly. "I've been waiting for an opening for thirty minutes."

Colleen smiled. "Meet me out there, okay?" Kevin nodded, and Colleen gave him a quick wave goodbye.

As she started down the steps, Luke fell in beside her.

"Let me be the first one to wish you happy birthday," he told her.

"Thanks," she said gratefully. "I can't believe I'm turning eighteen."

"It's gonna be a heck of a year," he said to her. "I hope we'll get a chance to get to know one another in the future as well as we know one another in the past."

Colleen's breath caught involuntarily in her throat as Luke's hand brushed against her right shoulder. He turned without explanation to head back into the boathouse.

She and Luke did have this cosmic connection. She couldn't deny it. Why should she deny it?

In that moment, as she went down the steps to join the others around the New Year's bonfire blazing in the backyard, her heart felt like a piece of steel caught between two equally powerful magnets.

Betsy pressed in next to her. "Happy New Year, Belmont," she said. "And Happy Birthday."

"Not for ten minutes," Colleen reminded her, pointing at her watch. "Let me enjoy my youth a little longer."

"Where's Kevin?" Betsy asked.

"Bathroom. He'll be out in a minute. I hope. I guess."

"Colleen, is your heart doing that pinball thing again?"

"Am I a terrible person?" Colleen said softly.

"Human," Betsy surmised, as one of the junior guys took out a guitar and started to play softly. "Two guys per girl; I'd say that's the way the world is supposed to be."

Someone screamed.

Then more people screamed.

"Oh, very funny. *Scream, the Sequel to the Sequel to the Sequel*," Colleen quipped.

Then she gasped as she saw why everyone was screaming.

And then she ran as fast as she could back to the boathouse.

It was on fire; flames were shooting out of it everywhere. There were still people inside.

Including Kevin.

And Luke.

"Colleen, no!" Betsy bellowed.

But it was too late.

154

Colleen grabbed the wood-splitting ax that was sunk into a tree stump at the foot of the steps to the boathouse, and raced up the stairs. In the background, she could already hear the wail of the Lakeside Fire Department's two engine companies. An alarm had been sounded, and the fire station was merely a mile or so from where the Wus lived.

Colleen took the ax and smashed it into the front door of the boathouse. A wall of smoke and fire confronted her, but she was unstoppable. She stepped into the burning building, dropped to the ground, and crawled forward, knowing that Kevin and Luke were both inside.

The fire raged and crackled around her as she inched her way forward. She coughed uncontrollably, her face blackened by the smoke and soot. Still, she crawled.

She felt a body with her right hand.

Kevin.

She felt another body with her left hand.

Luke.

Both of them were facedown on the floor, gasping, unable to move.

Oh, my god. Which to save? I can't save them both! OH, MY GOD! I CAN ONLY SAVE ONE OF THEM! WHICH DO I SAVE, KEVIN OR LUKE?

She had heard people talk about how, in moments of life-threatening crisis, time slowed down to milliseconds and their lives flashed in front of their eyes. But it had never happened to her.

Until that instant.

But instead of her life flashing in front of her eyes, her past lives flashed by.

The London Blitz.

The Civil War.

The Blizzard of '88.

Colleen grabbed at a body. The decision had been made.

With superhuman strength, she hoisted herself up, flung him over her shoulders, and staggered out of the building just as the asbestos-suited firefighters ran up the stairs and hoses began pouring water on the inferno behind her.

"Colleen! Oh, my god!" Betsy cried. "Help her! Help!"

Colleen fell to the ground under the weight of the body she carried, coughing and choking. A paramedic grabbed her and pressed an oxygen mask to her face, ordering her to breathe. Another couple of paramedics tried to revive the boy whose life she had tried to save.

She fought the paramedic's hands, swearing that she was okay. Was he alive? Wild-eyed, she scrambled to her feet.

"Don't die on me!" she screamed, running to the paramedics gathered around the prone boy. "Oh, God, please don't die on me!"

sixteen

℘

"*K*evin," Colleen prayed softly, "I love you so much. God, please take care of him and make him well. Please."

Colleen sat in an ugly plastic chair in the waiting area of Lakeside Hospital's emergency room, her dad's arms around her shoulders, and prayed for Kevin's recovery. The room was full of people, all waiting to hear about Kevin's condition, and many of them had their eyes closed and were praying as well.

Colleen's and Kevin's families were there, as were Betsy, Brandon, and many of the other people who had been at the party. Even Tolliver and the Curls had come along to join the vigil for the injured boy.

Colleen had recovered quickly, and her parents had brought her a change of clothes to the hospital. But it had been more than an hour since they'd brought Kevin in, and the doctors still hadn't given them any news.

Betsy sat down next to Colleen "How you doing?"

"Okay," Colleen whispered. Her throat was raw and sore from smoke inhalation, her eyes swollen and bloodshot.

"I can't believe Luke is dead," Betsy said.

The paramedics had worked on Luke in the back of the ambulance all the way to the hospital. But it was too late. The nurse said that so far they'd been unable to reach anyone at Luke's home to notify them.

"I keep thinking this is a nightmare and I'm going to wake up," Betsy told Colleen. Her eyes were red, too, from crying. Now tears filled them again. "How could the boathouse have caught on fire? What if it's something I did? I should have checked the smoke alarm—"

"I don't know how the fire started," Colleen croaked, "but I know it wasn't your fault."

Betsy fisted the tears off her cheeks. "Kevin has to make it. He has to."

"He's going to live," Colleen insisted fiercely.

Betsy nodded and took her friend's hand.

"I don't know how I could have been so blind, Betsy," Colleen went on. "I was never in love with Luke. I was just blinded by being so attracted to him. But that isn't love. It's just lust. I didn't really know him at all."

"Here, sweetie, this should feel good on your throat." Mrs. Belmont handed Colleen a paper cup of hot chocolate she'd gotten from a vending machine.

"Want a candy bar or an ice cream?" Kat offered. "I'll get you anything you want."

Colleen shook her head no.

Kat hovered over her. "I couldn't stand it if anything happened to you."

Colleen smiled at her little sister. Kat had on jeans and a pretty new red sweater she'd bought at the mall. And she reeked of too much Sunset Magic perfume.

"I'm okay," Colleen assured her. "Honest."

"Some birthday," Betsy told Colleen glumly, trying for a wan smile. "It's two in the morning, which means you've been eighteen for two whole hours now."

A terrible thought hit Colleen.

"Oh, God, Bets. Maybe I was supposed to die in that fire, right at midnight."

"No," Betsy said.

"Yes!" Colleen panicked. "Maybe Dr. Rathsmussen was wrong, and we were right all along. Maybe I'm *still* going to die!"

Betsy said nothing. She was as scared as Colleen.

"What are you two talking about?" Mr. Belmont asked.

Colleen had told her parents a lot about her regressions.

But she'd left out the parts where she died.

Now, she told them everything.

"—and it's happening again," Colleen finished, trembling with fear. "Luke is dead. Kevin might die. Which means I'm going to die, too! I've got to get home, I have to get someplace safe, before something terrible happens to me!"

She jumped to her feet, but her father grabbed her and hugged her, and over her head, raised his eyebrows at his wife. She nodded at him and then shrugged.

"First of all, Colleen," her father said, restraining her, "that woo-woo stuff is utter nonsense."

"That's what Kevin says," Colleen said, struggling to get loose. "But—"

"And second of all," her mom went on, "your birthday isn't January first."

Colleen dropped her arms. *"What?"*

"What?" Betsy and Kat echoed.

"The truth is, sweetie, your birthday is December

159

thirty-first," her mom admitted. "You were born at eleven-fifty-six P.M., four minutes before midnight. Your father and I were so happy and giddy, and . . ."

"Probably a little crazy, too," Mr. Belmont put in.

Her mother nodded. "We started talking about how if your birthday was New Year's Eve it would always be overlooked. When I was a kid, my best friend's birthday was on Christmas. She always got birthday/Christmas presents. Everyone was too busy celebrating Christmas to celebrate her birthday. I always felt bad for her."

"So, we just fudged a little," her father said, "and pretended with you that your birth was a few minutes later."

"So you see, you got a birthday that wasn't New Year's Eve," her mother said, "and your father got the tax deduction for the year you were actually born in."

"I was pretty pleased with that," Mr. Belmont said. "I'm glad your mother pushed so hard!"

Betsy whirled on Colleen. "Don't you see? You already lived through your birthday!" She exhaled loudly. "I gotta tell you, I'm relieved."

"Me, too," Colleen admitted. She looked at her parents. "It's strange to think you guys could keep a secret like that from me."

Kat screwed up her face. "My parents are very weird."

"I suppose that's true, Kat," her father said, giving her a hug. "But they're the only ones you've got."

At that moment, Betsy's parents came rushing in through the emergency room's doors. They'd been at home, dealing with the firefighters.

"What?" Betsy asked, jumping up. "Is everything okay?"

"It's fine," her mother said. "We just wanted to come see how Kevin was doing."

"They still haven't told us anything," Betsy said.

"The fire is completely out now," Mr. Wu said. "We wanted to tell you what the fire chief told us. It looks as if it was arson."

"*What?*" Betsy screeched.

"He thinks someone spread gasoline around inside the boathouse, then lit it," Mrs. Wu said.

"Who would do something that sick?" Colleen asked.

Mrs. Wu looked at Colleen. "I know Luke was a friend of yours—Betsy told me. Did he smoke?"

"I know he didn't," Colleen rasped. "I remember him saying so."

"The paramedics found a lighter in his pocket," Mrs. Wu said.

"No," Colleen said slowly. "It can't be."

"Yes, it can," a voice said. It was Tolliver. He was standing near them, and he'd heard everything. "I tried to warn you at the party, Colleen, remember? The guy seemed rather strange to me, and I decided to do a little research. So I hired a private detective. The guy was a paranoid schizophrenic. He assaulted the boyfriend of a girl he liked when he was fourteen, then he threatened the girl's life. Supposedly, he was okay if he took his medications. I guess he didn't."

Several of the kids had gathered around as Tolliver was speaking, and a buzz went through the crowd.

"That can't be right, Tolliver," Colleen protested. "Maybe I didn't really love him. But he and I shared lifetimes together before this. We did!"

"Does anyone know if smoke inhalation can make you crazy?" the Curls asked dryly. A couple of people tittered.

"Go ahead, laugh," Colleen said. "But Luke knew everything about every one of my past life regressions. He could only know if he was there."

"Uh . . . maybe not," Kat said sheepishly.

Everyone turned to her, and she edged closer to her sister.

"I know you told me not to look at the personal stuff you write on your computer," Kat said as quietly as she could, "but I kinda did. A few nights ago I was reading about your regression stuff and someone hacked into your machine through your modem. I went to your Telecom program, and the hacker's phone number was there. I recognized it."

She fished in her back pocket and brought out a scrap of paper. A phone number was on it. "It was Luke's number. I recognized it from when I wrote it down for you that time that he called." She handed it to Colleen.

"So Luke read everything you wrote about your regressions," Betsy figured. "That's how he knew."

Kat looked unbelievably sheepish, and tears pooled in her eyes. "I know I should have told you. But I figured you'd kill me for sneaking into your files after you told me not to. And I thought Luke was your friend. Is it all my fault?"

"No," Colleen said. She hugged her sister. "I know you would have told me if you thought he was dangerous."

Kat nodded miserably. "I'm really sorry."

"Excuse me, where are Mr. and Mrs. Armour?" a nurse asked, coming over to them.

"They went to the hospital chapel, I believe," Tollie reported. "They said that—oh wait, there they are."

Kevin's parents walked wearily into the waiting room.

"Dr. Slavik would like to speak with you," she told them.

"Is Kevin—" Mrs. Armour said, her voice trembling.

Colleen got up and joined Kevin's parents, taking his mother's hand for support.

Dr. Slavik, bald and middle-aged, came over to them. "Mr. and Mrs. Armour, I'm happy to tell you that it looks as if Kevin will be okay."

"Kevin!" Colleen cried. Happiness filled her like a helium balloon.

"Thank God!" Mrs. Armour almost fell over from relief. Her husband and Colleen steadied her.

"He took in quite a bit of smoke," the doctor continued, "but his burns are mostly first and second degree, not as serious as we first thought, and luckily his face was pretty much spared. His heart and lungs are strong and sound. We have a terrific burn unit here. He'll be well taken care of."

"Thank you, Doctor," Mrs. Armour said. "Thank you so much."

The doctor smiled. "You're welcome. I'm glad I can bring you good news."

"Can we see him?" Mr. Armour asked.

"Briefly," Dr. Slavik warned. "He has to rest. Who's Colleen?"

"I am," Colleen said.

"He's asking for you," Dr. Slavik said. "He made me promise to let you come in so he could tell you something."

Colleen gave Kevin's parents a questioning look.

"Go," his mother said, smoothing Colleen's hair. "We'll go right after you."

"Thank you." Colleen hugged Kevin's mother, then she hurried down the corridor to Kevin's room.

He was hooked up to a million machines, and his arms were covered with burns. His face was black and red, his eyes swollen, his hair and eyelashes singed.

But he was the most beautiful thing Colleen had ever seen. Because he was Kevin. Alive.

"Hi," she said tenderly, looking down at him.

"Have to tell you. Luke set . . . fire . . . to kill me."

"I know that now," Colleen said. "He was sick, Kevin. I'm so sorry I didn't know before. I'm so sorry."

"You saved . . . my life," Kevin rasped. "Not his."

"When it was a matter of life and death, it was all so clear to me. I love you, Kevin. Only you. With all my heart."

He managed a small smile. "How . . . many . . . lifetimes?"

She laughed through her tears. "All of them, I hope."

"Happy Birthday," he whispered. "Love you, too. Forever."

"Beyond forever," Colleen said. And her heart filled with joy, because at last she knew it was true.

Cherie Bennett often writes on teen themes. This novel is her latest for Avon Flare, which also published her popular *Teen Angels* series written with her husband, Jeff Gottesfeld. She also wrote *The Haunted Heart* in the "Enchanted Hearts" series.

Cherie writes both paperback *(Sunset Island* and *Pageant* series, *Searching for David's Heart)* and hardcover fiction *(Life in the Fat Lane, Zink)* for young people. Her Copley News Service syndicated teen advice column, "Hey, Cherie!" appears in newspapers coast-to-coast. She is also one of America's finest young playwrights and a back-to-back winner of The Kennedy Center's "New Visions/New Voices" playwriting award.

Cherie and Jeff live in Nashville, Tennessee, and Los Angeles, California, and can always be contacted at P.O. Box 150326, Nashville, TN 37215, or e-mail at **authorchik@aol.com**.

READ ONE...READ THEM ALL—
The Hot New Series about Falling in Love

MAKING OUT

by KATHERINE APPLEGATE